SWEET TILLY

A Drifters and Dreamers Romance

Other books by Carolyn Brown:

Love Is
A Falling Star
All the Way from Texas
The Yard Rose
The Ivy Tree
Lily's White Lace
That Way Again
The Wager
Trouble in Paradise
The PMS Club

The *Drifters and Dreamers Romance* Series:

Morning Glory

The *Love's Valley Historical Romance* Series:

Redemption
Choices
Absolution
Chances
Promises

The *Promised Land Romance* Series:

Willow
Velvet
Gypsy
Garnet
Augusta

The *Land Rush Romance* Series:

Emma's Folly
Violet's Wish
Maggie's Mistake
Just Grace

SWEET TILLY

•

Carolyn Brown

AVALON BOOKS
NEW YORK

Published by Thomas Bouregy & Co., Inc.
160 Madison Avenue, New York, NY 10016

Library of Congress Cataloging-in-Publication Data

Brown, Carolyn, 1948–
    Sweet Tilly / Carolyn Brown.
        p. cm.
    ISBN 978-0-8034-9857-0 (acid-free paper)   1. Single
women—Fiction.   2. Sheriffs—Fiction.   3. Healdton
(Okla.)—Fiction.   I. Title.

    PS3552.R685275S94   2007
    813'.54—dc22

                                                    2007016633

PRINTED IN THE UNITED STATES OF AMERICA
ON ACID-FREE PAPER
BY HADDON CRAFTSMEN, BLOOMSBURG, PENNSYLVANIA

In memory of my stepfather
Ebb Essary
who entertained us with stories
about making 'shine.

Chapter One

Tilly Anderson wrapped her arms around her knees and drew them up to her chin, staring out between the bars of the jail cell at the new sheriff. Rayford Sloan. Irish by name but those were Indian cheekbones. Having grown up with her grandmother, Katy Anderson, she knew Indian when she saw it. The high, chiseled cheekbones, black ebony eyes under dark lashes. Black Irish? Maybe a little with a name like Sloan. Indian? Definitely. The lips were a combination, though. Full. Sensuous. Soft. Tempting. She focused on a soft-looking mouth, one that she'd like to get to know much better. She blushed at that idea and wondered where in the hell it had come from. Ever kissing Sheriff Sloan was completely out of the question. She'd do better to be attracted to Lucifer, himself, than the sheriff of Healdton, Oklahoma.

However, watching him kept her mind off the

1

mattress beneath her, the lingering combination of too many Saturday night drunks, rat urine, and stale sweat. If she kept herself drawn up into a tiny ball, perhaps there would be no evidence that she'd ever been in this place when Tucker came to rescue her. She focused on the sheriff again. His trousers fit snugly around his narrow hips, his shirt tight on his broad shoulders. If she narrowed her eyes she could imagine muscles rippling beneath the soft chambray shirt. He had to be somewhere around her age . . . early thirties. Yet, his face said he'd lived longer. Seen more. Been more places. Etched into those high cheekbones were stories she'd love to hear. Personal ones. And Tilly didn't figure they were all sugar-and-spice tales either.

"What are you staring at?" His tone matched his dark hair, worn a little too long. His near black eyes, dark, with no warmth. Somber, with no humor. His color was jet black.

She'd always matched a person with a color. That made them easier to understand. Clara, her cousin, was light blue, soft and sweet. Bessie, down at the Morning Glory Inn, an elderly woman she'd adopted as another grandmother years ago, was pink. Beulah, the other new owner of the inn was lilac. Libby, Clara's new daughter, was bright yellow, like a ray of sunshine. Tilly figured she was red. Bright red. Bold. Sassy. Didn't give a damn what people thought. Red, that was Matilda Jane Anderson.

"Sheriff, the first lesson you'd best learn if you want to keep that bright new shiny badge is not to corner something meaner than you are," Tilly said in a silky smooth, Southern voice.

"And you think you are meaner than I am?" The sheriff raised a heavy, jet-black eyebrow at the snippet of a woman behind the bars. Dark hair, eyes the color of a blue summer sky; looks that would have gotten her burned at the stake three centuries before because no decent woman could be that pretty naturally. She'd have had to have used spells and sorcery. Chills tickled up and down his spine, but he held her stare, not backing down for an instant.

"Oh, honey, it's not even a contest," she whispered.

"Yep, it's a fact that you are definitely cornered. But, I don't think I've got anything to be afraid of in the likes of a common moonshiner." He propped his legs up on the desk and combed his thick black hair with his fingertips. "This time tomorrow that fancy car you got out there with *Sweet Tilly* on the big heavy plate coverin' the radiator will be mine. And if I can uncover a still on your property, it'll be mine too. The whole farm, not just the still." Lord Almighty, he'd locked up seasoned hookers that were terrified of him out in east Texas. Tilly Anderson acted like she was on a Sunday afternoon picnic, not a drop of fear in those icy cold blue eyes. She might be half witch after all.

"Sheriff Sloan?" The door swung open and another woman filled the space, the sunrise silhouetting her, but leaving no doubt that Clara Anderson Nelson had come to town to rescue her cousin. She was taller than Tilly but the two of them stood the same. Ramrod straight. Confidence oozing out their pores like sweat on a hot July day. Clara left no doubt she'd attempt to put out a forest fire with a bucket of water. She was only a little less daunting than her shorter cousin, who the sheriff figured would expect a forest fire to die if she spit on it.

"Mrs. Nelson?" Rayford Sloan slowly slid his feet from the desk and stood up.

The tap of her boots made a *rat-a-tat* across the wooden floor. Despite the early morning hour, her dark hair was piled up on top of her head and she was dressed like she'd just come from a Sunday afternoon social. "I've come to see exactly why Tilly is behind bars." She pulled off snow white gloves and propped one hand on her hip, the other on his desk as she leaned toward him.

"Matilda Anderson was caught in a moonshine car with a whole load of empty fruit jars. She's a moonshiner," he said.

"Darlin', did you open those jars and smell them? Did you run your tongue all around the inside to make sure there was moonshine in them?" Tilly asked.

"Of course not," the sheriff barked. Damn, she looked like a queen. Even wearing men's overalls, rolled up at the hem and a size too large, and a flannel shirt. Sitting on a tick mattress, behind bars. She could have used a broom handle as a scepter and men would have fallen all over themselves to be the one she selected to break her out of jail. Whoever the unlucky fool was, he'd go to the gallows with a smile on his face and an ethereal look in his eyes.

"Then how do you know they held moonshine?"

Clara asked. "Sounds to me like you made a big mistake, Sheriff Sloan. Tilly was bringing those jars to me to can soup in this week."

"Oh really. I know where your farm is, Clara Nelson. And I know where Tucker lives and where Matilda lives. Why would she be out at one o'clock in the morning coming from Wirt to bring you jars?"

"Tilly?" Clara walked closer so she could see her cousin.

Tilly sighed. "I put the jars in my car yesterday. Figured I'd take them to Clara's after church this morning. I decided to drive over to Wirt and check on a sick friend. There is no law against driving around with a bunch of empty jars, is there, Sheriff Sloan? You want to point out chapter and verse to me in the law book that says, 'Thou shalt not put fruit jars in the back seat of thy car'?"

"Why didn't you tell me that story when I stopped you last night?" Rayford set his mouth in a firm line, jaw muscles doing double-time.

"You didn't ask me." Tilly didn't move from her position on the bare, straw tick mattress. "You saw the jars, the metal plate covering up the radiator and the back of my car with no seats and decided I was guilty of moonshining."

"You are willing to vouch for her?" Rayford asked Clara.

"I'm not vouching for her, Sheriff. I'm just telling you the truth." Clara didn't flinch or look away from his piercing black eyes.

Rayford prided himself on being able to tell when a

person was telling the truth. There was no way that woman was lying. Yet, he had a gut feeling that he wasn't wrong either. Tilly Anderson had been running 'shine and those jars in the back of her specially outfitted automobile were filled with illegal liquor at one time. He didn't need to run his tongue around the rims. He felt color creeping into his neck just thinking about the way she'd set his senses on fire when she'd mentioned it. He hadn't thought about the jars but rather her full, lush mouth and how it would feel to run his tongue around those lips. To wrap her up in his arms and kiss her until she admitted that she was a moonshiner.

"You are a lucky woman." Rayford picked up the key ring and opened the jail cell. "You are free to go."

"Don't think so, darlin'," Tilly inhaled deeply.

"Tilly!" Clara glared at her cousin.

"What do you mean?" Rayford asked.

"I was hauled in here in the middle of the night. Afraid to go to sleep for fear rats or roaches would carry me off. Both of them are big as bobcats in this place. What do you feed them anyway? Must keep them fattened up on something and you didn't offer me even so much as a single drink of water. Nothing to do but sit here and stare at your mean old hateful face through the bars. I think you owe me an apology, Sheriff Sloan. When I get it, I'll leave your jail."

The door sounded like a shotgun blast when he slammed it shut. Every fiber in his body was tense with anger, every nerve raw. Angels would sell moonshine in heaven before he apologized to that woman.

"Tilly, you come out of that cell right now," Clara said, swinging the door open.

"Oh, Clara, I was just joking with the good sheriff." Tilly put her feet on the floor and stretched, arms straight up, neck wiggling out the kinks. "He sure doesn't have much of a sense of humor, does he? Looks like he was weaned on a dill pickle, don't he? Don't look at me like that, Clara, darlin'. Let's go see what Dulcie is cooking for breakfast."

"It's Sunday morning and I've got a child to get ready for church. You can come home with me. Flora is making omelets. Does she need to sign anything?" Clara asked the sheriff.

"Not a thing," he growled.

"Good day, Sheriff Rayford Sloan. Maybe I'll see you in church after a while. If you sit beside me on the back pew, please nudge me if I fall asleep. After all, I haven't had a wink all night." Tilly dillydallied beside his desk.

"Get out of here," he snarled.

"Oh, my feelings are hurt now as well as my pride," Tilly said.

Clara sighed.

"I'm going to lock you back in there if you don't leave," he declared.

Tilly pulled up a chair and sat down in front of his desk, leaning forward toward him. "I thought we could be friends, even if we did get off on the wrong foot. You were wrong. Admit it."

"I'm going home, Tilly. If you want breakfast you'd better be following me," Clara told her.

"I am hungry and someone has to look after you when you drive. Why on earth Briar ever gave you your own automobile is a mystery. I thought he loved you and he goes and buys you a car. Now there, Sheriff, is a crime worth locking a man up for. She doesn't pay a bit of attention to the road when she drives. Looks like she's been making trips to the woodshed to sample the moonshine, the way she weaves from one side to the other. You ought to arrest Briar for premeditated murder. She's going to kill herself and whoever is riding with her." Tilly made no attempt to get out of the chair.

"Tilly!"

"I'm coming. See you later, Sheriff, and darlin', don't be droolin' over my Model T out there. It'll snow in hell the day you and that badge take my car." She nodded curtly at the man.

"Oh, yes you will definitely see me later, Miss Matilda Anderson. You will see me every time you turn around, every time you sneeze or cough. I'll know what you had for dinner thirty minutes after you eat, and if you run 'shine in my town, I will catch you. I'm still not convinced that you are a sweet innocent farmer who was out to see a friend last night. So I'll be the shadow behind you. And if I smell a drop of 'shine in that car, it will be mine."

"Remember what I said. Don't corner something meaner than you are," she whispered and leaned forward so close the warmth of her breath caressed his lips as gently as if she'd brushed a kiss across them.

Before he could form an intelligent sentence in his befuddled mind she was gone. But he'd sure meant what he said. He'd shadow her until he had her behind bars for more than a night. The whole town would see who was the meanest.

"Tilly, what in the world was you thinking?" Clara leaned against the new Model T her husband, Briar, had bought her the week after their wedding the previous month.

"He made me mad. I just tilted his halo a little bit. Good old boy that he is, he'll get it straightened up before long. How did you get here so quick anyway?"

"Dulcie saw your car parked out front and looked in the windows. Saw the jars in the back and peeked in the windows of the sheriff's office. Saw you sitting in the cell. She got Nellie to drive out to the farm to get me."

"Well, bless her heart. I'm going on home but I'll see y'all in church this morning. Wouldn't give that man in there, or anyone in town who knows I spent a night in jail, the satisfaction of thinking I wasn't innocent."

"You'd pass up Flora's omelets?" Clara couldn't believe her ears. Tilly had made noises about stealing Clara's cook, Flora. She came to dinner so often these days that Flora didn't even ask about setting an extra plate.

"This morning, I'd better. I've got to take a shower and wash my hair before church. Get all the jail off me."

"Okay, I'll see you in church." Clara nodded.

"Thanks for vouching for me." Tilly hugged her cousin.

"Why, darlin', I wasn't vouchin' for you. I was tellin' the truth. Come tomorrow morning you'll have those jars on my kitchen table for Flora to can soup in." Clara smiled.

"You've got jars a plenty at your house," Tilly argued.

"Yes, but Flora is canning soup in those jars. That way if the sheriff shadows my house he'll see I was telling the truth. So you bring them to me right after church. Like you told the good man in there, don't corner something meaner than you are."

"Clara Anderson Nelson, you ain't never seen the day you could whip me for meanness." Tilly laughed.

"The jars, Tilly. That's my price for coming down here before breakfast."

"They'll be there. I promise. Small enough price to pay for freedom, I guess."

Rayford Sloan paced the floor after Tilly left. Few men had gotten under his thick hide in the thirty-five years of his life. He'd never allowed a woman to upset him as much as Tilly Anderson had. He hadn't planned on going to church that morning. Not after pulling an all-nighter chasing down information he'd been given about the woman running moonshine for a living. One thing for sure, he'd be a lot more careful about the news Inez from the drugstore passed on to him. She'd set him up for a big embarrassment. Telling him in hushed tones that Matilda Anderson's grandmother had run liquor. That she'd learned the trade from her grandmother, who'd been involved with the great whiskey rebellion more than a hundred years before. Melvin Anderson had married Katy Evening Star Hawk, but it was years before he knew the part Indian, part Irish woman was a moonshiner. Rumor had it that she taught her daughter-in-law the trade. That would be Tilly's mother. By the time Oklahoma came into the union as a dry state, Tilly Anderson had already been taught the art from the women in her family. Of course, according to Inez, no one could prove a word of it, but everyone knew.

Rayford had a feeling that the story was gospel quality even if he hadn't gotten a conviction. He glared at the open cell door. He'd catch her next time with full jars instead of empty ones. He'd catch her taking money from a buyer with the goods in one hand and a fistful of dollars in the other. By damn, if it took every ounce of his energy, Tilly Anderson was going to be locked up in prison and he would get to own that fancy new car. That would be his prize for taking her down. Instead of selling it at auction and keeping the money for himself like the law declared he could if he caught her and she was convicted of running illegal liquor, he'd keep it and drive it all over town. He might even leave that ridiculous radiator cover on it. The one that had her name engraved in fancy script . . . *Sweet Tilly*. Well, if that woman was sweet, Lucifer had a halo and a set of pure white wings.

Tilly parked her Model T in front of the barn, pulled a key from the pocket of her overalls as she slid out of the seat, opened the padlock and threw open the doors. She checked the lane to make sure the sheriff hadn't made good on his word and started shadowing her every move right that moment. Surely she'd made him mad enough he'd have to work it out of his system before he even thought about following her around. At least she hoped that was the case. She began to unload six wooden boxes holding a dozen empty quart fruit jars in each. When they were all inside the barn, she shut the doors and threw a slide bolt from the inside.

She moved six bales of hay and opened a hidden door. A narrow staircase led from the door down into a basement below the barn. It was there that she carried the jars, one box at a time. Setting them on a work bench, she removed the lids and carefully smelled each of them. Sparkling clean. Just like she demanded from her customers. The new sheriff had thought she was pulling his leg when she asked him if he'd licked the inside rims of her jars. She wasn't.

She checked the temperature of the mash and the still. Granny Anderson had taught her well when she told her making the 'shine was the easy part. Outrunning the revenuers was the difficult part of the business. That and keeping your identity as secret as possible. Granny and Matilda's mother both had been so careful that no one could ever prove those two women weren't churchgoing saints. There were ways to make, package, and sell without ever being discovered.

Katy Evening Star Anderson had fallen quite naturally in her ancestors' footsteps the first time her mother took her to the basement beneath the barn. Stills already in place. Nice underground cold stream to provide the water source. Perfect place to make mountain dew. That's what her grandmother called it back in Pennsylvania. Folks around southern Oklahoma referred to it as 'shine or white lightning. Some called it stump liquor because a shiner would leave the product on a stump out away from town. The buyer would take the moonshine and leave payment on the stump. It didn't matter what they labeled it, it was spelled m-o-n-e-y. Recipes varied and were top secret. Katy Anderson's didn't call for a drop of yeast. Patience was the key, she'd told Tilly when she was teaching her the technique. Better to let the mash brew for the full ten days than rush it with yeast and have it finished in three days. Smoother 'shine was the result. Keep the current customers happy and you didn't have to spend all your time out hunting for new ones.

The last of Katy's original customers died last year. The last one who knew for an absolute one hundred percent bonafide fact who the runner was that supplied his shine. Tilly worked the system the same way as the old stump payers. She took the 'shine in the back door of the establishment, left it on a shelf or in a closet, picked up her money and empty jars, and disappeared into the night. If anyone did see her they'd figure her for a half-grown boy out running around after dark.

If Tilly Anderson got caught, it wouldn't be with a bottle of 'shine in one hand and a roll of bills in the other. No sir, she'd paid closer attention to the lessons from her mother and grandmother than that. She hadn't lived to be thirty years old by being careless. And if Sheriff Rayford Sloan wanted to shadow her, he'd better get ready to lose the chase of his life.

Chapter Two

Tilly slipped into the church just as the congregation began the first hymn. Clara, Briar, and Libby were sitting on the back pew so she slid in beside them and shared a songbook with Clara.

Libby leaned forward, pink ribbon streamers tangled up in her dark curls. She wore a burgundy dress with pink trim, little shiny black shoes and pink socks. She dropped one eye shut in a perfect wink. Tilly smiled and winked back. That child could easily be Clara's by birth rather than adoption. If her cousin birthed ten children by the time she was forty, there would never be another who'd be more like her.

Briar nodded at Tilly. A handsome man in a rugged sort of way. The exact opposite of what she'd figured would appeal to her cousin. But the heartstrings don't often listen to the brain cells when it comes to love. After the fight that lasted all spring and summer, Briar and Clara had finally admitted they were miserable without each other and had gotten married a few weeks before.

Clara looked the radiant bride even after a whole month. The stylish dark blue dress she wore would make all the women in the church envious. But it was the light in her blue eyes and the lilt in her voice that Tilly envied. The happiness. The love that surrounded her like a misty aura. Tilly wanted that for herself, but there was only one Briar Nelson and he'd fallen in love with Clara.

"Got boxes of fruit jars in the back of my car. Not the same ones but you can still go to heaven," Tilly whispered into her cousin's ear.

Clara suppressed a smile and kept singing. It didn't matter which jars Tilly brought, but she wasn't about to tell her cousin that. Tilly looked like a vision out of a catalog in the soft blue dress she wore that morning. The exact same shade as her eyes, and the hat she'd chosen sported one of her famous little half veils, stopping at her chin, covering little, promising everything. Clara looked over the eligible men in the church. Which one could lift the veil and find the real Tilly underneath? Not the preacher with his prissy ways. Good lord, Tilly would eat him for breakfast and spit out the bones on her way to the barn to check the mash. One of the oil men who worked for Briar? Maybe. But it would take a special one.

Tilly caught the twitch in the edges of Clara's mouth and almost missed the next note. She dearly loved her cousins, both of them. Tucker was just barely a month older than Tilly; Clara, a month younger. They'd all three been raised together like siblings. The wild Anderson cousins in Healdton, Oklahoma. Clara had hated all things that had to do with the oil boom, but somehow her heart failed to get the message and last spring fate had put Briar Nelson, an oil man, right in her path. She couldn't get around him. Couldn't go over him or under him. Finally ended up falling in love with the man and his daughter, Libby, who now called Clara "Momma."

After the hymn the preacher took his place behind the podium. He cleared his throat seriously and opened his Bible. Silence spread out over the congregation like a cloud of cigarette smoke in a bar over in Wirt. He squared his shoulders and narrowed his eyes, looking out over the people as if his word, and his alone, held them in the balance between heaven and hell. For effect, he kept them in total suspense for a full minute before he looked up toward the ceiling in a silent moment of prayer. Theatrics, yes. But he'd been taught by an expert to keep the congregation in the palm of his hand. And as long as he held them there, he had a job.

"Today I'm going to speak again about the evils of moonshine," he began in a loud booming voice that made several children jump, a couple of elderly men jerk open their eyes from the nap they'd planned to take, and a few women nod in agreement.

Tilly rolled her eyes. It was his favorite topic. He'd preached against the wiles of drinking at least twice in the last month. Most likely, since she was the most prosperous moonshiner in the whole county, he'd heard the stories and had taken it upon himself to re-habilitate her through preaching. He might as well ser-monize against something else, like not coveting your neighbor's donkey, because there weren't enough words in the Good Book to make her change her way of life.

Sheriff Rayford Sloan eased in the back door and tapped Tilly on the shoulder, motioning her to scoot down the pew so he could sit down. He'd promised her a shadow. There was no time like the present to begin.

His touch sent a jolt of fire slicing through her heart. As she made room for him, she rationalized it was because she'd had thoughts in jail that morning about kissing him. She ignored the way his arm brushed against hers in the close quarters, or at least she attempted to overlook it. She kept her eyes on the preacher. Watched him take a clean white handker-chief from his coat pocket and mop sweat from his brow. Watched him sling his hands around to make his points. And didn't hear a word he said.

Rayford Sloan had shaved. There was a small dot of blood right below his right ear. He wore freshly ironed trousers and a leather vest with his bright sher-iff badge pinned above his heart. He'd applied some kind of shaving lotion that reminded Tilly of pure masculinity every time she inhaled. His jet-black hair, worn a little longer than most men and attesting to the fact that there was a bit of rebellious Indian in his blood, was brushed straight back and his profile was nothing but downright sexy.

When the preacher wound down and asked an elderly man to do the benediction, Clara leaned over and whispered, "He needs to smile more. He's so serious, he makes me sleepy."

"Who?" Tilly asked.

"Julius. The preacher," Clara answered. So Tilly hadn't been paying a bit of attention. Must be the sheriff who'd kept her mind from that long, boring sermon. Now there was a man who might tame her cousin, but the two of them were beyond the realm of possibility. They'd kill each other.

"He can't smile," Tilly whispered back. "That's the first step into the flaming bowels of hell. Don't you know there's a special book in the Bible for preachers? In it, there's a verse that says, 'Thou shalt be serious or scorch in hell.'"

Clara slapped playfully at her arm. "Shhhhh." She put her finger over her mouth.

Rayford wondered what the soft buzzing of whispers concerned. All he caught was something about the flaming bowels of hell. Most likely Miss Tilly Anderson was telling her cousin where she wished the sheriff would spend eternity. Personally, he didn't care what the woman thought and the preacher couldn't have done a better job if Rayford had begged for the message to be about moonshining. It must have taken every ounce of Tilly's self-control to keep from squirming under the heat of the sermon.

"Mornin', Ford." Briar reached across his wife and Tilly to shake hands as they waited to get out of the church. "Got plans for dinner? You could come home with us. Our cook, Flora, had the house smelling like baked ham by the time we left."

"And Tilly is coming. And Tucker is too," Libby piped up in her sweet four-year-old voice. "They always come to Sunday dinner at our house."

"I wouldn't miss it for anything," the sheriff said and grinned at the child.

"How wonderful," Tilly said through clenched teeth and a fake smile. "Well, since you're going, you might as well ride with me. Get a little taste of riding in a car you'll never own. What does a person call you? Rayford? Ford? Sheriff? Lawman?"

"Thank you, Miss Anderson. I'd be happy to ride with you. Folks call me all of the above. My mother called me Ford unless she was angry, then it was my entire name. You can call me sir," the sheriff said sarcastically.

"Don't hold your breath until I call you sir, lawman. You made it clear we are not going to be friends so I'll just be the exception to the rule and call you Ford anyway. I'm glad you're riding with me. That way you can unload those jars you were so concerned about last night," she snapped right back at him.

"My pleasure."

"Try licking the inside of them. You might like the taste of last year's peaches," she whispered seductively.

"Love peaches." He barely moved his lips but the way his eyes twinkled let her know the battle lines had definitely been drawn. Just as surely as if he'd drawn a line in the dirt out on the main street of town and put his toes on one side, daring her to step across.

"Well, that's settled," Briar nodded. "We'll see both of you at the house in a few minutes. Clara, why is Tilly bringing jars to the house?"

Clara pinched his arm. "I told you yesterday, sweetheart. Flora and I are canning soup tomorrow."

"Yes, ma'am," Briar chuckled. "Jars for canning soup. You did tell me at the breakfast table this morning. Forgive me, darlin'. I still have trouble listening to you. When you're in front of me, well . . ."

"That means the honeymoon isn't over," Tilly said. "If you're going with me, lawman, you'd best come on."

"Well, hello, Miss Anderson. You are looking lovely today, as usual." The preacher beamed as he took Tilly's hand in his.

"And he smiles. You must be Lucifer's cousin, enticing him down to the bowels of hell," Clara whispered right behind Tilly.

"Thank you, kind sir." Tilly slipped her hand from his clammy palm. "The service was uplifting this morning."

"Ahh, yes." The preacher continued to smile. "Well, we must rid ourselves of this big blight on society called moonshining. Of course, you wouldn't know anything about such a thing. Not a lovely lady like you."

The sheriff choked behind her.

"Some folks aren't as trusting as you," Tilly said seriously, shooting the sheriff a look meant to drop him in his tracks right there in front of God, the preacher, and the whole town. "This man actually made me spend the night in jail because he thought I was running illegal liquor." She pointed at the sheriff.

"Oh, dear. Well," the preacher flushed bright red, "I'm glad it was a mistake."

"Why don't you come to dinner with us," Libby said in a loud voice right beside Tilly. "The sheriff is going to come and see my kittens. I could show them to you too."

"If you don't have plans," Clara looked the preacher right in the eye, "we'd be glad to have you." It would serve her cousin right to be smacked down in between the sheriff and the preacher. That would be justifiable atonement for Clara having to rush around so early that morning, not to mention having to tell that blatant lie.

"I'd be glad to join you," the preacher told Clara, but his eyes never left Tilly.

"Could we give you a ride?" Briar asked.

"No, I'll need to drive my own rig. I have some sick folks to visit this afternoon out that way. It would be easier if I take my horse and buggy," he said.

"I'll get even," Tilly sing-songed under her breath as she walked out of the church beside Clara.

"I don't care," Clara retorted in the same whiny voice.

"Well, lawman," Tilly turned to the sheriff not ten feet behind her deep in conversation with Briar, "do you need to tell anyone at the office you are going to be away for dinner, or are you ready?"

"I'm ready," he said.

The jars clattered together as they rode out of Healdton toward Briar and Clara's farm. A message reminding Ford Sloan that he had a job to do, no matter how lovely the Miss Matilda Anderson was. The same noise on a soap box in Clara's mind, telling Tilly loudly that the good sheriff was the enemy. No matter if he smelled good and his lips begged to be kissed. He wasn't about to put her out of business, but he definitely would take her farm and that was the most important part of what had been left to her. The music created behind the seats was written for words that said, "Leave the man alone. He'll be your ruination."

"Tell me, Tilly, do you use yeast in your recipe and a little brown sugar?" the sheriff asked out of the clear blue, hoping to catch her off guard.

"Yeast, always. But I use white sugar. Brown sugar would never work." She kept her eyes on the road and the twitch in her mouth under control.

"You admit right here that you make the recipe? Of course, it's just your word against mine since there are no witnesses, and honey, I will haul you into jail again."

"Admit that I make the recipe with yeast and white sugar? Yes, I'm a good cook. Now Clara, she never learned to cook, but darlin', she can play the piano like a pro. I'm surprised she never went to New York and played in the big time. Granny Anderson taught me and Tucker to cook. Clara just never could get the hang of it. But she's musical and she can clean a house until it glows."

"Then you do make moonshine, and use yeast and white sugar?" Ford Sloan could scarcely believe that she owned up to her profession.

"Moonshine? Good Lord, man, are you still on that? I'm talking about the recipe for good homemade bread. I thought that's what you were talking about too. Yeast bread. With white sugar, not brown."

"You knew exactly what I was talking about," Ford growled.

"No, you said the recipe with yeast. Well, that's the only one I use yeast for. Homemade bread. Let it rise up a couple of times. Make it out into loaves. I make really good bread. Someday you'll have to sample it. Sometimes I bring it to the spring church picnic. Think you'll still be around next spring or will you have this end of the county all cleaned out by then?" She parked in the front yard, beside Tucker's truck.

"Oh, I'll be here. By Christmas I'll own your car and your farm so I won't have a reason to leave."

"Darlin', don't hold your breath until that happens. I don't reckon you'd look good in that shade of blue." She didn't wait for him to open the door but bailed out and went inside the house, leaving him to fend for himself.

"Where is Ford?" Briar came down the stairs, his coat and tie off, shirt sleeves rolled up to the elbows.

"He's a big boy. He can find his own way inside." Tilly passed him on the steps as she headed up to the bathroom.

"Riled you wrong did he?"

"No, I'm in love with the man. He's a prince on a big white horse and I'm the princess in the tower."

"You're in love with Ford?" Clara opened the door to her bedroom and peeked out.

"No, I am most certainly not. He's a pompous . . ." Tilly stammered looking for the right word. "He's the north end of a southbound broken down workhorse."

Clara shook her head and shut the door.

"Come right in, Ford. I'll go find a couple of glasses of iced tea to sip on while we wait for lunch. Julius should be along soon. Guess you passed him on the way?" Briar's voice carried up the stairs.

"Come right in Ford," Tilly whispered, snarling her nose like an eight-year-old girl at the woman in the mirror above the bathroom sink. She removed her hat and hung it on the hook high on the door. "Come right in and connive your way into the hearts of Tucker and Briar and hope you can use them to get to me. Come right in Ford but be aware I really am mean when I'm cornered."

"Who are you talking to in there?" Clara asked.

"Myself," Tilly threw open the bathroom door. "I'm hungry. I hope Julius doesn't take too long cleaning his wings and adjusting his halo. Men! Can't live with them and they'll hang you for killing one of the worthless critters."

"Ford is getting under your skin is he?" Clara looped her arm in Tilly's and the two of them went downstairs together.

"That lawman. No, ma'am. He doesn't have what it takes to get under my skin. He's just making me mad, that's all."

Ford and Briar waited for them in the living room. Sunshine poured through the windows across the shiny hardwood floor. Not a particle of dust could be found anywhere. Not on the piano, the mantle above the fireplace, or even the multitude of small tables scattered about the room. Tilly noticed there was a little bit on Ford's boots. He'd better be careful or Clara would be hunting up a dusting rag to take care of that problem.

"Ladies." Briar's face lit up when he saw Clara. "Flora just left. She said the table is set and the food is ready to be served. We're just waiting on Julius. We should petition the deacons at the next financial meeting to buy an automobile for the good preacher. That way he could get around faster."

"I'd vote against it," Tilly said.

"Why?" Ford asked.

"If he wants a car, he can buy it himself," Tilly said.

"But you're not a deacon or a member of the financial committee, are you?"

"No, I'm not. But someday they'll let women fill those places. We've got more common sense than men and we'd do a better job of it."

"Guess you think you're big enough to be a sheriff too?"

"Yes, I am, but you can keep the job. I don't want it."

Sparks bounced around the room searching for a place to land. Clara and Briar could feel the tension between Tilly and Ford, and smiled at each other, remembering the previous spring when they'd first gotten to know each other. But Clara was not a 'shine runner and Briar hadn't been a sheriff.

"Anybody want to see the babies?" Libby brought a picnic basket into the living room, alive with squirming kittens. "There's a yellow one," she picked up a fluffy ball of fur and deposited .it on Tilly's lap. "That's Aunt Tilly's favorite one. His name is Boots 'cause he's got four white feet. And here's one you can hold." She handed Ford a solid black one. "Her name is Midnight but she's not a bad-luck cat. Momma says she's a good little kitty, and even if she gets hair on your britches it won't show. And the other one is Flower because she's got lots of colors on her." She cuddled a calico to her own breast. "Momma says I can keep them all so don't you be lovin' on Midnight too much," she admonished Ford.

"Yes, ma'am." Ford rubbed the kitten behind the ears. "She looks like a pretty good cat to me, Miss Libby. I bet she'll grow up and be a good mouser."

"That's what Aunt Tilly says. She says black cats are mean and can catch a mouse real fast. I hope she does and eats it all up. I hate mice. They scare me," Libby said.

"How old are you?" Ford asked.

"I'm four and Uncle Tucker and Momma and Aunt Tilly are all thirty this year. Are you old?"

Briar chuckled. Clara blushed. Tilly laughed aloud.

"Guess I am. I'll be thirty-five on my next birthday," Ford said seriously.

"That's really old. Do you remember dinosaurs? Momma is reading me a book about dinosaurs."

"No, can't say I do remember them." Ford frowned at Tilly.

"Well, I'm trying to find somebody old like you who can still remember. I want to know what they smelled like. Now give me back the babies and I'll take them back to their momma. She's going to tell them a story." She shoved them back into the basket.

"There's Julius," Briar heard the rig coming up the lane about the same time Libby slammed the back door.

"Come on, Clara, I'll help you get dinner carried to the table," Tilly said. "I'm starving."

"You're always hungry. Ford, don't ever offer to take this woman out to dinner. She'll break you."

"On my salary, a bowl of beans would break me," he said.

"Then darlin', you'd best not set your eyes on Matilda Jane Anderson. She likes to eat," Tilly said sarcastically.

"Don't reckon I'd set my eyes on you anyway, Miss Anderson. You've got too sharp a tongue for this old lawman."

Clara pulled Tilly out of the room and into the hall-way before her temper exploded and the flames caught the curtains on fire. "Come on. He's trying to rile you. If he can, he's got the power over you and it won't be long until he'll use that power to put you right back in jail. If you want to get the best of him, you'll have to keep a cool head."

"You are right," Tilly said, a plan formulating in her mind. It would take some serious thought, but it could work, and it would smear mud all over the sheriff's face and tarnish his shiny badge. To be bested by a woman would be the best revenge for sitting in a jail cell all night.

Briar occupied the head of the massive oak dining

table with Clara to his right and Libby on his left. Tilly sat beside Libby with Julius on her other side and Ford right across the table. Tucker, the other cousin, a serious-looking man with dark hair and blue eyes that looked as if they could pierce pure steel, occupied the space at the end of the table.

"Missed you in church this morning, Tucker. Thought I might have to put you on my sick visiting list for the afternoon," Julius said when he finished delivering a lengthy grace.

"I'm not sick. Had a dozen cows break through the fence and wander out last night. Had to get them in and missed church." Tucker stuck his fork in an enormous slab of ham and laid it on his plate. "Flora got a good sting on the ham," he said after the first bite.

"What does that mean? She didn't sting the ham, Uncle Tucker. She just cooked it in the oven," Libby said.

"It means it's cooked perfect." Tucker smiled at the child. She'd already wrapped the whole family around her fingers. All she had to do was blink those blue eyes and he and Tilly both were struck senseless.

"Okay," Libby said.

"Well, you missed a good sermon. Julius preached on the evils of moonshining," Ford said.

Tucker swallowed hard to keep from choking. "It does seem to be a problem," he said after he'd downed half a glass of iced tea.

"Yes, it is. If we are ever to get this area respectable, we must start at the bottom and root out the culprits that are making and supplying illegal liquor."

Julius helped himself to a double portion of sweet potatoes, topped with brown sugar and pecans.

"I agree," Ford said, looking across the table at Tilly.

"Aunt Tilly, tell the preacher where you got your name. He doesn't know about your Granny." Libby shook her head when the sweet potatoes came her way.

"Why?" Ford asked.

" 'Cause her name comes from that stuff you're talkin' about," Libby said.

"Moonshining?" The preacher frowned and turned to look at Tilly.

"I'll tell the story," Tucker said.

Tilly almost blushed. "No, let me. After all, it is my name. You see, Julius, my grandmother Anderson, Katy Evening Star Hawk Anderson, was a moonshiner. A real one. Her grandmother was involved with the great whiskey rebellion you read about in history. She made liquor and distributed it all over this part of the country. My grandfather didn't even know about it for many years. Her grandmother taught her mother the art. Her mother taught her. Granny said she and Grandpa never needed the money but she just couldn't stop making liquor so she put all her money in the bank. When each of her three sons married, she gave them a right nice present. She bought Tucker's daddy and mother the farm he lives on. Tucker's mother named the farm The Evening Star after Granny. She bought Clara's folks the house she had in town, the place she turned into a bed and breakfast. The Morning Glory Inn. Named that because Granny loved morning glories even better than roses. My farm is the original old homestead. Mother loved Granny and became the daughter she never had."

"Nice bit of history, but what about your name?" Ford asked.

"Granny's grandmother had two old mules she used to pull the wagon she delivered the 'shine in. No one expected a fine upstanding churchgoing woman of making stump liquor so she never got caught. Or even suspected. Anyway, one mule was Matilda. One was Jane. When her mother took over the business, she kept the mules until they died and she replaced them with two horses. One was Matilda. One was Jane. When Granny had to replace the horses, she named them Matilda and Jane. Only she shortened them to Tilly and Janey. And she had *Sweet Tilly* painted in bright red letters on her buggy. The one she delivered her stump liquor in. When Mother delivered me and I was a girl, Granny wanted to name me Matilda Jane. Three generations of 'shine-pulling horses and mules had been good to our family. So Mother let Granny name me."

"Fitting," Ford said.

"And why is that?" She glared across the table at him.

"You're as stubborn as a mule."

"Takes one to know one."

"Someday I'm going to have a little girl, and I'm going to name her Midnight Flower after my cats," Libby said, breaking the tension.

"So the business died with your grandmother?" Julius asked amid the laughter.

"I told you it was passed from mother to daughter. All my grandmother had was three sons and they are all dead." Tilly fluttered her lashes at the preacher.

He blushed crimson. "I'm sorry. All of your parents are deceased?"

"Yes, they are. The famous Galveston hurricane took both of Tilly's parents. She was thirteen and they'd gone down there for a holiday. Thank goodness they had left her with Granny. You should have heard the hissy fit she threw at being left behind. Tucker and I heard about it until we threatened to stop talking to her. My father was a banker and dropped with a sudden heart attack years ago. Mother died when I was nineteen. I kept up the boardinghouse until a month ago. Tucker's mother died with the fever when we were all eleven, and his father was killed in a hunting accident when Tucker was eighteen," Clara told him. "Enough about the Anderson kids. What about you, Ford? Where did you come from? Planning on staying in Healdton?"

"Oh, no. Only about a year. That's all it takes to clean up an oil boomtown. That's what I do. I came from east Texas. And I'll move on. I'm just a drifter."

"Me too," Briar said. "At least I thought I was until I met Clara."

"And me," Julius said. "Just drifting through and helping Ford. He does the physical work. I do the mental. We're a team."

"So were you in east Texas too?" Tucker asked.

"Oh, no, I came here from Memphis, Tennessee. My father is a preacher. Both my grandfathers were preachers, and their fathers before them. But I'm a drifter too. I clean up towns and move on to the next one when the Lord says my work is finished."

"That's what is so strange about you," Tilly said aloud before thinking. "It's your voice."

"My voice?" Julius asked.

"Yes. At church, it's big and booming. Now it's different." She eyed him.

"Where did that come from?" Ford asked. He'd noticed the difference in the man's tone long before today.

"Just hit me," Tilly said.

"A preacher can keep his congregation's attention if he has a preaching voice, so my father taught me to both lower my voice and raise the volume," Julius explained. "Excellent meal, Clara. Tell Flora she's outdone herself."

"I'll be sure and do so." Clara nodded.

He's a good-looking fake, Tilly thought. One way behind the podium. Another outside the doors of the church. At least the lawman is the same no matter where a person sees him. Obnoxious. Tacky. Determined. Dependable. Even if he is out to get me.

Chapter Three

The door to the library squeaked when Ford opened it. He'd hoped to sneak in without being noticed amongst the crowd of silly women, but someone had forgotten to oil the hinges on the door. Everything and everyone went silent as a morgue. The crowd was not even a dozen strong and the room was smaller than he'd anticipated. He'd pictured all libraries to be just like the one in Deport, Texas. A big desk near the front door and rows and rows of books. This one was one small room with makeshift bookcases lined up around three walls. The books looked old and well worn.

Several women sat in a semicircle around a podium where Tilly held down several loose-leaf pages with her hand and glared at him. Briar Nelson and Tucker Anderson slouched in a couple of chairs behind the women. They looked as out of place as a couple of hookers standing in front of St. Peter. But they were stoic. At least they weren't fidgeting like Libby who sat beside her father.

"Sheriff, what can we do for you?" Tilly asked.

"Thought I'd sit in on the meeting," he answered.

"Do you enjoy poetry?" Clara asked.

"Don't know. Guess I'll find out," he said, working his way back to an empty seat beside Libby.

"You don't care about poetry. You are harassing me," Tilly said flatly.

Nellie coughed to cover a giggle.

Clara gasped.

"Probably, but from what I understand the public is invited to this meeting. So I'll just sit back here and listen to you read your little poems and make sure that's all that goes on in these meetings. We wouldn't want you leading all these other good women down the path of destruction or attempting to coerce them into helping you in your journey from riches to rags."

"Well, the lawman has a poet's heart hiding behind his shiny little star. Such a way with words, I wouldn't be surprised that he doesn't write a novel. I hope you enjoy the free verse of T. S. Eliot, a new poet. I was about to read 'Cousin Nancy' from *Prufrock and Other Observations*," she said. Her heart skipped around in her chest like a second grader on school recess, but she'd confront a rattlesnake rather than let Ford Sloan know he'd ruined her evening.

She dragged up a smile from the depths of her soul and went on with the poem about Miss Nancy Ellicott who smoked and danced and her aunts who weren't sure how they felt about it, but considered Nancy quite modern, anyway.

"That's not a poem," Ford said when she'd finished.

"Why, because it doesn't rhyme or because it's about a woman who's modern and does what she wants in spite of what people or family think?" Tilly fired back.

"It's not a poem because it doesn't rhyme. Poems rhyme and you read them like they do. You didn't even read it like a poem. You read it like it was a piece of prose," Ford argued.

"Eliot is a new poet," Nellie said. "He's quite popular and what we're studying tonight has just been published. He writes in free verse, just like Tilly told you when you came in."

Briar sighed. If Ford kept arguing and expressing his opinion they'd be there until midnight. Libby squirmed in the seat beside him and eyed the refreshment table. Her father wished he was four and could get away with the same thing.

Tucker sat up straighter. It could get interesting after all. He remembered the first night Briar came to a reading. That was when Clara found out he was an oil man and tried to force the sheriff to help her evict him from The Morning Glory Inn. She failed and he stayed, but in the end everything worked out wonderfully well. He eyed Ford and Tilly. Could it be? *Lord, no!* His inner voice exclaimed. *Not a sheriff and a moonshine runner. They'd either kill each other or one of them would have to give up their profession.*

"Anything else?" Tilly's voice dripped sarcasm.

"No, just expressing my opinion. Is it over?" Ford grinned. He'd accomplished exactly what he wanted. He'd riled her. He didn't think for a minute that she'd be running 'shine at a poetry reading, but it would force her to realize he intended to make good on his word about shadowing every move she made.

"No, it's not over. It's barely begun. Are you sure you want to stay?" she asked.

"I'm tough. I can endure it." He slumped down in the chair and crossed his arms over this chest.

"We'll discuss the modern ideas of this poem and Nellie will be reading one entitled 'Aunt Helen,' and after that Cornelia is presenting 'Morning at the Window.' You sure you can stand to hear something different?"

"Just wake me if I fall asleep. Are those refreshments for afterward?" Ford raised an eyebrow and glanced toward the fancy table off to one side.

"Yes, they are." Tilly was exasperated and her tone couldn't cover it any longer.

"I expect they'll make up for the dryness of the reading. Continue on ladies. I'll just sit back here with Briar and Tucker and try to stay awake," Ford said.

Boredom set in quickly. Tucker and Briar seemed to be sleeping with their eyes open. Libby kept crossing her blue eyes and tilting her head to one side or the other. Ford tried it once but two of Tilly Anderson was one too many. Finally, he studied the women who were intent upon Eliot's poetry. Nellie, the old maid school teacher, who lived at the Morning Glory Inn. Cornelia, the other teacher at the Healdton elementary school. Not as old maidish as Nellie, but not far behind. Clara, a lovely woman, who'd owned the Morning Glory for years. Until she met and married Briar. Ford had thought about renting a room there and more than likely Bessie or Beulah, the two new owners and managers, would have been glad to have him. But he couldn't imagine living in a house with two gray-haired opinionated women, two school teachers who certainly didn't have a bit of problem speaking their minds, and a flighty, flirty lady by the name of Olivia, who chased everything that wore pants.

At exactly eight o'clock Briar and Tucker sat up a little straighter. Libby followed their lead and smiled at Tilly who took her place behind the podium and announced that if there was no further business, the meeting was adjourned and refreshments would be served.

"They're called the dreamers," Libby whispered to Ford.

"Who?" He leaned down closer to the little girl.

"All of the ladies and even Uncle Tucker. That's what they call the club. The dreamers. I think it's because they put Uncle Tucker and Daddy to sleep and make them dream."

"You are probably right." He smiled. "Let's go have some cookies and punch."

"Aunt Tilly made them. She makes the best oatmeal raisin cookies in the whole world. Momma made the punch, though. She makes good punch since Flora taught her how. Someday she's going to cook, but Daddy says she don't have to if she don't want to. Flora cooks for us. I like her," Libby said as she grabbed Ford's hand and tugged him toward the refreshment table.

"Surprise, surprise," Tilly said as she handed him a crystal cup of punch. "It's just plain fruit juices with a little almond extract to cut the sweet. I understand extract is partially alcohol so maybe you'll want to take us all to jail for the night since we are partaking of alcohol. You do have a place for children since I intend to let Libby have some and she'll no doubt be as drunk as the rest of us."

"Very good. I do believe that extract is legal since when you buy it you do pay the proper amount of tax and it's not considered moonshine." He held out his cup for a refill before he moved on down the line, picking up cookies on the way.

"What are you going to do about that man?" Clara whispered.

"Outrun him," Tilly retorted. "But tonight I've got to go to Wirt. It's absolutely essential since he's really going to harass the devil out of me. Think you can keep him occupied?"

"Oh, sure." Clara tolled her eyes. "You'd do better to get him into a discussion with Nellie and Cornelia. They could bend his ear for hours. You will be careful, won't you?"

"I'm not delivering anything but messages tonight. No jars in the back. None to bring home. He won't catch me with a single thing but pencil and paper. I don't think he can throw me in that stinky jail cell for that."

"Just be careful. You should have shut down the business a long time ago. Now that Sheriff Sloan is on your trail like a bloodhound after a coyote, things are even more dangerous, Tilly."

"I'm not stopping because of him. He don't scare me one bit, and by the time that sorry drifter rides out of Healdton, he's going to realize he can't outsmart me, either."

"And what are you ladies discussing so seriously?" Briar slipped his arm around Clara's waist and drew her close.

"Whether or not to make chocolate cookies or a cake for the next reading," Tilly said glibly.

"I'd vote for a cake. A big old three-tiered chocolate one with chocolate filling and thick icing. I could sit through the dullest of poets for a wide chunk of that." Ford joined the group. He'd been watching Clara and Tilly, deep in conversation no one could hear across the room where Nellie and Cornelia had crawled up on a soap box about women's rights.

"That's what it will be if you want one," Clara said. "I'll be in charge of it."

"But Momma, you can't cook something like that," Libby said as she picked up another cookie.

"No, but Flora can." Clara laughed. "And I bet she'll let us both lick the frosting bowl."

"Yeah!" Libby shouted. "I'm going to go tell Uncle Tucker. He might even stay awake next time." She dashed off to the other side of the room where the women had him cornered.

"I'm turning in early tonight." Tilly managed a fake yawn. "We still on for supper tomorrow night?" She ignored Ford and looked at Clara.

"Sure. Supper at six. Why don't you join us?" Clara turned to Ford.

"Love to." Ford nodded. He could easily get used to eating real often at Clara and Briar's place. Besides, he liked Libby and her fresh outlook on everything. Oh, to be four again, when everything in the world was a wonder. He could endure Tilly's sarcasm and barbed remarks for a good meal. At least she'd be in the room with him and not out running 'shine all over the county.

"I'll see you at six." Tilly carefully placed her punch cup on the table. She would have rather thrown it at Ford's grinning face. It appeared that she wasn't going to be able to go to the outhouse without coming out to find him leaning on the door.

Clara nodded and asked Ford if he was truly coming to another poetry reading. "I do declare, I never thought Tucker would keep up with the evenings once Tilly and I were old enough not to need a chaperone. I think maybe he likes them more than he admits, though. Poor Briar doesn't know a poem from an oil report so he just tolerates them."

"Small price to pay to get to watch you and listen to that lovely voice." Briar flirted openly with his wife.

"I'm with Briar. You ladies do have nice voices," Ford said. He squinted through the dark window, following Tilly as she got into her car and roared out of town. True enough to her word, she did go in the direction of her farm, so he thanked the ladies for the evening and sauntered back toward the jail.

Everything was quiet in town. No one occupied

either cell, so he climbed the stairs on the west side of the building and went up to his apartment. Two rooms shabbily furnished. They'd said they'd provide room and board and give him a salary that was equal to his last job. Board was whatever the hotel cook sent over when he had prisoners or else he ate in the dining room when the jail was empty. Room was what he opened the door to. A small living room–bedroom combination. The iron bedstead and springs were only slightly better than those in the jail cells. The mattress had more lumps than his Grandmother Sloan's oatmeal. A rocking chair and chest of drawers completed what came with the room. Sloan's roll-top trunk had been pushed up to the end of the bed. He'd decided years before that what would fit into that trunk was all he needed. Anything more would be extra baggage. No material possessions and for sure no relationships to keep him in one spot long enough to put down roots. No sir, Rayford Sloan was a free spirit. One-quarter Indian. One-quarter Irish. And the rest a healthy mongrel mixture, none of which would ever settle down in one place.

What was supposed to be a kitchen and dining area was through the narrow door to the left of the only window in the bedroom. A wood stove, which he used for cooking and no doubt would be depended on all winter for heat, took up most of the space. A table with two mismatched chairs held a few pots and pans and dishes. Enough for one person to cook a pot of beans and eat them from something other than the black cast-iron kettle. Not that he'd done any cooking since he'd taken the job. Not even a fried egg or piece of toast. Or that he planned to fix a meal for himself, either. As bad as it was, the hotel food would always outshine anything he could cook. At that business, he and Clara Anderson had a lot in common.

He stared out the bare kitchen window. A sheriff didn't need curtains on the window, nor did he have the impulsive obsession to keep it clean, so he had to focus his eyes past years' worth of dust and grime. A full moon lit up the street, not like daylight but pretty close. With that much light there was no mistaking the glittering sign on the front of Tilly's car as she eased carefully back through town. He laughed aloud. So she was going home to call it an early night. Horse-feathers! She was out running 'shine right under his nose and she'd laugh about it tomorrow. He hurried back down the steps and jumped into the sheriff's car, following her toward Wirt. He could see well enough by the light of the moon, so he didn't turn on the lights. She wouldn't even know he was behind her until she opened up the car doors and began toting liquor into the bars. He could stop her at any moment, but he'd rather have her either with full jars in her hands or else a bottle in one hand and payment in the other. Excitement filled his breast as he thought about bringing her in. No doubt about it, he'd forfeit his invitation to dinner the next night at Clara's, but he'd own the Sweet Tilly by morning.

She drove straight to Wirt and parked in an alley behind Lucky's place, a pool hall where men gathered supposedly to play poker and listen to music provided by a local jazz band. Men who worked the oil fields by day and played for a few extra dollars in the evening. Everyone knew that more than Coca-Cola or iced tea was served in the place. It was the first place on Ford's list to shut down but so far he hadn't been any luckier than the other lawmen who'd tried to catch Lucky serving bootleg whiskey.

Ford drove on past the alley, parked as soon as he could, and ran back to the edge of the building. He peeped around the edge. Tilly took her own time about getting out of the car, stretched and wiggled the kinks from her neck. So this was her first stop when she was out delivering. He waited for her to take a wooden box filled with full quart jars from the car, but she didn't even look back. She went in a back door and in less than a minute she came back with the same thing she'd taken inside in her hands—nothing.

Frustrated, he watched her get into her car and back out of the alley, not even noticing him standing in the dark shadows not five feet from her as she drove away. He hurried to his own vehicle, turned it around, and followed the taillights back toward Healdton. What was she up to? Nothing went in. Nothing came out. Did she know he'd follow her and was simply taking him on a joyride? Couldn't be. If she didn't sell moonshine, what was she doing going in and out the back door of a well-known joint?

By the time Tilly got back to Healdton, she knew Ford was tailing her. He hadn't interfered with her mission in Wirt, so hopefully, he'd think she was jerking him around and leading him on a wild goose chase.

She drove straight through town and kept going east. If he wanted to confront her, by golly, he could do it, but he couldn't lock her up for riding around in the middle of the night, chasing in the back doors of poker clubs, now could he? Her next stop was in Hewitt, at a two-story house where five ladies lived. The kind of women who did their business after the sun went down. Well-known in the area and one Ford really wanted to close the doors on. She opened the back screen door and again was in and out before he could get his vehicle turned around.

She tried to ignore the bulky dark figure outlined by the full moon, but it was still there every time she checked the mirror. What must he think? Or did he think at all. Maybe he was tormenting her like she must be aggravating him. Only she was on a mission and he was just playing the shadow game.

Ford followed her to Dillard where she parked behind a house that appeared to be a residence. When she opened the back door and disappeared inside, again for only a minute, he had no doubt she was toying with him. But she didn't know that he'd figured her out and she'd be madder'n hell at him for keeping his word about keeping her in his sights at all times. So he'd keep up with the game until she went home.

Her next stop was at the Hotel Ardmore where she seemed to know exactly where the back door was. She looked around before she dashed in and out and he had to jump backward to keep from being spotted. People's houses. A brothel. A hotel. A joint in Wirt. Where on earth was she going next?

She answered his question by driving to Wilson and making a run into another brothel and into the backdoor of the hotel. One thing for sure, the woman had lots of acquaintances or else she was one brazen hussy, just going into people's homes and businesses without even knocking. When she left the hotel, she drove back to Healdton and made a stop at the hotel there before she drove straight to her farm. He watched from the end of the lane as she parked her car beside the house. Lights lit up the windows just inside the front door. In a moment, they went out and two windows on the second floor went from pitch black to warm yellow. Evidently she'd led him all over the county and the game was over. He went home to his two tacky little rooms, threw himself on the bed and stared at the ceiling. Brothels could have orders for moonshine. Probably did. So did the joint out in Ragtown. But the Hotel Ardmore. He didn't think so. That place wouldn't endanger their business for a little illegal liquor. Neither would the hotel in Healdton or the one in Wilson. It had all been a hoax to tease him.

Tilly threw off her clothes and ran a bath. She was bone tired from the tension, half expecting Ford to stop her any minute and demand an explanation as to what a churchgoing woman was out doing all night. She eased down into the hot water, glad her Granny had insisted on having the first indoor bathroom in the whole town. Now all she had to do was keep Ford at Clara's tomorrow night until the plan was completed. She shut her eyes and dozed. When she awoke the water was cold and had a soap scum on the top. She shivered as she rinsed her skin and wrapped up in a towel. She turned the lights off and fell into bed, the soft clean sheets feeling good against her bare hide. There was nothing she'd like better than drifting off to sleep, but she still had work to do before daylight.

When she was sure she'd given the good sheriff enough time to get back to Healdton, she made herself push the covers back and with a sigh, crawled out of bed. She groped in the dark for a flannel shirt and her overalls, dressed in the dark, pulling her boots on at the top of the stairs. Congratulating herself on making it from the foyer through the living room, dining room, and kitchen without turning on a light, she opened the back door and went to the barn.

She didn't use a lantern there either, depending on her instincts to take her down to the basement where she carefully picked up the first box of full jars. Five trips later she had them all in the back of her car. Without turning on the lights she drove carefully into Healdton, avoiding the main street, circling most of the town and stopped in the middle of the cemetery. An abandoned old wooden caretaker's implement shed was the place she unloaded the boxes. Each with a note attached to the side of the box about where the next week's delivery would be dropped.

Once upon a time, folks had called moonshine or stump liquor. Folks would leave their shine on a stump and the buyer would pick it up and leave the money. If it worked for the old-timers, it should work for Tilly. While her customers picked up the merchandise, she'd be at Clara and Briar's house, having supper with the sheriff himself. If he'd been following her, he would have already stepped out of the darkness and confronted her. Now all she had to worry about was someone discovering what was in the old shed. Surely kids wouldn't be playing hide-and-seek in the cemetery on a school night.

It was near daylight when she left her overalls and shirt in a pile on the floor beside the bed and sank back down into the beckoning arms of a feather mattress. She dreamed of the lawman finding her stash and pouring it all out.

Chapter Four

Tilly dressed carefully in a red dress trimmed with black buttons and pin tucks down the bodice. She pulled her dark hair back into a bun at the nape of her neck and tugged a few strands loose to float around her face so she didn't look so much like an old maid. "But that's what I am," she said seriously as she slipped her feet into shoes. "An old maid. Every man in town, except the obnoxious preacher and the even worse sheriff, is already married and has a house full of kids. At least the men who might interest me. I could find a husband down in the hobo villages, but I'm serious. I want what Clara has."

She'd plowed most of the afternoon, getting the ground ready for winter wheat, so she was grateful for the invitation to have supper with Briar and Clara. Good food. Good company. She'd ignore the lawman. Hopefully, he would show up. Even though she'd kept him up until the wee hours of the morning, he needed to be there. Otherwise, someone might go running into his office, telling about an unusual amount of traffic in the cemetery.

She didn't realize she was holding her breath until she parked in the driveway and saw him sitting on the porch swing with Libby, kittens all over his lap. She exhaled heavily and bit the inside of her lip to keep from grinning. Now all she had to worry about was getting to her payments with him watching. She'd outsmart him and he'd never know. That was truly revenge for having to sit in the jail all night.

"Aunt Tilly!" Libby came running as fast as her chubby four-year-old legs could carry her. She wrapped her arms around Tilly's legs and hugged her tightly. "Come and see my kittens. The sheriff has played with them long enough. You can have a turn now."

"Evening, Miss Anderson," Ford said from the swing when she let Libby lead her up to the porch.

"Sheriff." She nodded.

"Have a seat. There's room for three." He patted the swing.

"I think I'll go on in and help Clara get the table set," she declined.

"Afraid of me?"

"Not in your wildest dreams," she threw over her shoulder as she left him and Libby playing with kittens.

"Hi, darlin'. Is that lemon chicken I smell?" Tilly said at the kitchen door.

"Hello to you. Yes, it is. Flora got everything ready before she went home. How'd you do last night? I tried to keep him entertained until you got away." Clara carefully checked the dining room and cocked an ear toward the porch.

"He followed me to every stop. I think he figured I had him out on a wild goose chase after the way he crashed our poetry reading. Anyway, I left a note at each one telling them where they could pick up their merchandise tonight. Actually, this is going to work better. I'll deliver the goods and pick up my money. All I have to do is keep the lawman busy on the nights my customers are in town."

"Good Lord, Tilly. You're not having them come into Healdton, are you? They'll get caught and squeal like stuck pigs."

"No, they won't, because not one of them knows where the merchandise comes from. They may have an idea who their supplier is, but they couldn't prove it. All they know is it arrives on time and in good shape and they leave the money for the next week's delivery. Let's see if he's as smart as he thinks he is." Tilly grabbed a cookie from the counter. "I'm starving. This first night was a booger. I didn't get to bed until daylight."

"Tilly, give it up. You're richer than a whole oil company with all you've got your hands into. Don't put everything Granny left you in danger."

"No." she shook her head. "Maybe someday. But not now. I won't run from a battle. I've seen lawmen come and go. I'll be here when he's long gone."

"Be careful," Clara whispered as she nodded toward the front door where Briar was leading Ford into the house.

Briar kissed Clara on the forehead. "Give me a moment to wash up, honey, and we can have supper. Sorry I'm a few minutes late."

"I need to wash up, also," Ford said. Anything to stay out of the kitchen with two conniving women. Strange, how things worked out. He might have liked Tilly in another place, another time, another setting. He'd never been able to endure a whiny woman and Tilly surely did not stutter when she spoke her mind. He liked women with dark hair and Tilly had tresses that hung down her back. He could just imagine tangling his hands in all that hair while he kissed her senseless. Those blue eyes were an added bonus. The way they twinkled when she was up to mischief was nothing short of sexy. His ideal woman needed to be about four inches taller. As if that would ever matter anyway, because everything was all wrong.

"Follow me." Briar motioned toward Ford.

"I envy you." Tilly touched Libby's dark curls when she came through the kitchen.

"Libby, go put those kittens out on the back porch and come wash your hands. I'll help you get them clean right here at the sink. Your daddy and the sheriff are in the bathroom. Now why do you envy me?" Clara asked. "I never had the courage you've got, the determination, or the wild streak. I was the good girl who stayed home and kept a boardinghouse, remember?"

"Sure, until Briar came along and gave you an itch so deep you couldn't scratch it," Tilly said. "I'm jealous because you have got a wonderful husband, but most of all I'm jealous of Libby. Why don't you and

Briar give her to me? You can have more kids. A whole houseful. I won't ever even get one."

"Not on your life. That child is mine. Come on, Tilly. With your looks, you could have men standing in line outside your door just to be considered to father your children. Any one of them would marry you," Clara said.

"I don't want a husband. I just want a daughter," Tilly said.

"Sorry. Even Nellie and Cornelia haven't got a soap box big enough to preach that sermon. Society would crucify you. It's 1917 and we've come a long way, but it'll be years and years before a woman can have a daughter with no husband and get away with it. Not even you with all your brazenness can expect that."

"Guess not. But hells bells, it's what I want."

"And Sheriff Sloan wants your car. Think he's going to get it?"

"Over my dead body. But I see your point. Here, hand me that bread. I'll slice it and help you get things to the table. Think you can help me keep him here until late so there won't be a problem?"

"Smile and flirt. There's not a man in the world that would leave your side when you put on the charm."

Tilly shivered. "Charm a snake or get caught. Don't know which is worse."

"What's worse?" Libby and the two men arrived at the same time.

"Beets or onions?" Tilly kneeled down to look Libby in the eyes.

"Onions. They're stinky and they make Daddy's mouth smell terrible."

"See, just what I said. Onions are worse than beets," Tilly agreed.

"What am I, honey? An onion or a beet? Do I have layers of personality or am I just a big, dumb red lout?" Briar teased as he picked up a bowl of potato salad and took it to the table.

"You are a piece of triple layer chocolate cake." Clara smiled at him.

At that moment, Tilly blew the bottom out of the commandment about not coveting your neighbor's donkey. Not that she wanted Briar's mules or his cows. What she wanted was a love just like Clara had. With someone who looked at her like Briar did Clara. Someone who was a triple layer chocolate cake.

"And what am I? An onion or a beet?" Ford looked at Tilly.

"You, darlin', are neither."

"Since you called me *darlin'*, am I a chocolate cake?" He grabbed a big bowl of corn in one hand and a platter of chicken with the other.

"I call Tucker's ugliest mule *darlin'*. So don't go thinking that means anything. You are most certainly not chocolate cake. At best you might be a burned piece of cornbread that got thrown out in the backyard and the hounds refused to eat." She carried her platter of perfectly sliced bread to the table.

"Thank you so much. For a while I thought maybe you'd been flirting with me," he said.

"I'd come closer to flirting with that mule we just talked about so don't be worrying about me trying to end your bachelorhood. If you were the last man on earth, I fear the human species would die plumb out," she said.

"Ouch. You do have a tongue like a well-honed sword."

"Stay out of the kitchen if you can't take the heat." She drew out a dining room chair and seated herself.

"Children, children," Clara chided, reaching for Briar's hand. "Darlin', perhaps Tilly should say grace tonight. Looks like she needs to talk to God and sweeten up her attitude."

"Tilly?" Briar bit the inside of his lip. So they were sparring. That was the first step. But who'd give up what? Would Tilly stop her business? Would Ford stop his drifting ways?

"Dear Lord." She bowed her head and clasped her hands in her lap. "Accept our heartfelt thanks for this food and company gathered around the table tonight. I'll talk to you longer and in more depth later tonight. Amen."

"I like it when Aunt Tilly prays. She gets it over with," Libby said the second she heard the amen. "The preacher prays so long my stomach begins to cry."

"That must have hurt to give be nice and give thanks for the company around the table." Ford shot a look across the table at Tilly.

"You'll never know how much." Tilly reached for the chicken from Clara. "I do love Flora's lemon chicken. Someday I'm going to offer her twice the salary and steal her right out from under your nose." She deliberately changed the subject. She needed to keep him there until late in the evening and Granny always said flies could be caught much faster with honey than vinegar. Somehow in all her advice-giving, she never mentioned how many times a girl could get stung while gathering the honey to catch the stupid flies.

"I'll shoot you dead if you even think about stealing Flora," Clara said seriously. "Sisterly or even cousinly love only extends so far. And besides, there's not a better cook in the county than you, so you don't need her."

Tilly giggled and began to eat.

She was so beautiful when she smiled, when her face lit up in amusement, that it fairly well sucked all the air from Ford's lungs. Beauty beyond words. She could cook. Did the woman have flaws other than her sharp tongue and moonshining business?

"But Aunt Tilly can't clean. You ought to see her house. It would make Momma shudder," Libby said seriously, answering his silent question.

"Libby," Briar chided.

"Don't fuss at her," Tilly said. "She's right. I hate to clean. Someday I'm going to hire a maid. She's going to arrive every morning and stay until supper and do nothing but clean."

"You that dirty?" Ford asked.

"Yes, I am. Every time I think about a husband, I just take the man to my house. The last four joined the service and went to fight in the war to get away from me."

"Oh, Aunt Tilly, it's not that bad. I like your house. There's surprises hiding in the corners," Libby said.

"Along with dust bunnies, spiders, mice, and mold," Tilly said.

Ford's curiosity was piqued. Surely someone who was as meticulous about herself couldn't be that filthy of a housekeeper. Most women were naturally born cleaners, but he'd never known of a woman who actually ran a moonshine business alone and with enough finesse that no one really knew if it was rumor or not. So maybe she didn't make time to keep a spotless house.

"So you cook but you don't clean. You plow the fields and run your farm single-handed. It'd take a big man to buy into that," he said.

"Yes, it would. And I don't think God makes men like that anymore." She dabbed the corners of her mouth gently.

Manners too. She had impeccable manners, Ford noticed.

"Did He ever?" Briar asked.

"Oh, yes. But I think He tossed the mold out when He made you." Clara put in her two cents.

"Thank you, honey." Briar touched her hand.

"No thanks necessary. Only difference between me and Tilly is that she doesn't clean and I do. She cooks and I don't. Lots of men wouldn't get past the cooking problem. They'd listen to their stomachs rather than their hearts."

"How about you, Tilly? Think God will make a man big enough to tame you?" Ford asked.

"If He thinks a man can tame me, I expect He's got a surprise in store up there in Heaven. If He's working on one I can live with, He's got his work cut out for him. If He's got a mind to make one who will accept me He's got both hands and a wheelbarrow full of a job," Tilly said.

"Momma, will you play the piano after supper?" Libby changed the subject abruptly.

"I'll be glad to." Clara nodded. Maybe Ford would feel obliged to stay longer if they entertained him. Of course, the best way to keep him was for Tilly to start flirting and leading him on, but Clara didn't think that would happen until pigs sprouted wings and flew.

They'd barely finished the pecan pie for dessert and had their coffee when a heavy knock on the door made them all jump. Briar laid his napkin on the table and went in that direction, but another even heavier pounding commenced before he could make it out of the dining room. He found the part-time deputy on the porch, a worried look on his face.

"I need to talk to Sheriff Sloan," he said, his eyes darting from the sheriff's car back through the screen door. "It's an emergency."

"Ford, it's for you," Briar called out.

Ford was there by the time Briar finished the sentence.

"Sorry to bother you at supper time, sir, but we got us a problem. Red Johnson got drunk over in Ragtown today and come home just about the time the bank was closing. He went in there with a shotgun and robbed the place, grabbed that girl Olivia, the teller, as a hostage and dragged her out to his horse. Rode hell bent for leather out to his house and he's holed up in there. Says he'll kill her."

"Where's his house?" Ford was already going toward his three-year-old Model T.

"Right next door to the cemetery. Got a whole yard full of people out there watchin' the spectacle," Ralph told him.

"What's going on?" Tilly asked from the door.

"Red Johnson has taken Olivia, the teller at the bank, hostage. He's holed up at his house and threatening to kill her," Ford said as he jumped into his car and started the engine. "Leave the horse here and ride with me," he told the deputy.

"No, I'll bring the horse back and we won't have to make another trip out here. You can take care of it once you get there. He ain't listenin' to a word I've got to say anyway. That's why I rode after you." The deputy jumped into the saddle.

"Good Lord," Tilly exclaimed. She knew exactly where Red Johnson lived. Not a hundred yards from the shed where she'd left her stash the night before. "Briar, tell Clara where I'm going. I know Red. I might be able to talk sense to him."

She ate the sheriff's dust all the way back into town and left the poor deputy to breathe hers when she passed him riding as hard as he could on the sheriff's big black horse. She parked right behind Ford and looked back at the shed before she ran over to the edge of the lawn where people gathered to see what would happen.

"You haven't got a bit of business here. Go home," Ford growled at her.

"I know Red and Olivia is a friend. I can talk sense to him," she declared.

"You think I'm going to let you go in there and have

Red take another woman to kill, you are crazy." He stepped up in front of the crowd.

"Red Johnson, this is the sheriff talking to you. You turn that woman loose and come on out here."

A shotgun blast answered him. Men dropped to their knees. Women screamed. Tilly could have sworn the shot hit the shed. If that fool man broke those jars, she'd hang him herself.

"I ain't comin' outta here until I have a car and an hour head start. I'll leave this woman in Ardmore and someone can come and get her," he yelled through a broken window. "You come a step closer and the next shot will take you out instead of that old caretaker shack."

"I'm comin' in," Tilly yelled as she ran across the yard, across the porch and into the house before anyone could stop her.

"Now what'd you go and do that for?" Red said when Tilly burst into the living room.

"I'm just going to talk to you." Tilly sat down on the worn out settee beside Olivia who was wringing her hands. "This ain't right, Red. You wouldn't have done any of it if you hadn't been over there in Ragtown drinking all day. You'll draw some time for robbing the bank, but it won't be nothing like you'll get if you don't give yourself up."

"I ain't givin' in." Red spit a stream of tobacco onto the floor. His eyes bloodshot and his bulbous nose as deep red as his hair. "My woman done run off with one of them oil men. Took off down to Texas where they're drillin' next time. Now I got me two hostages, way I see it. Maybe I'll just tell 'em I want your fancy car."

"Ain't got enough gas in it to get you to the edge of town, but if you'll let Olivia go I'll let you have it." She kept an eye out the busted window toward the shack. No one saw a horse and buggy pull up and a man disappear inside, carry out a blanket-covered square box and leave. That would be the owner of the hotel right there in Healdton.

"You tellin' me the truth, Tilly? You wouldn't lie to ole Red would you? You really ain't got no gas in that car out there?" He squinted at her.

He was just barely taller than Tilly, scrawny enough that a good north wind could blow him all the way to south Texas. Tilly wondered how in the world he'd gotten Olivia up on that horse to tote her from the bank out to his house. She must have had a real dose of fear.

"I'm not lying to you, Red. It's barely got enough to get me back to my ranch. Stupid sheriff decided last night to follow me. Thinks I make moonshine so he's been shadowing me all over town. Even went to my poetry reading. So I took him on a wild goose chase all over this end of the county. Was nigh on to daylight when I finally got to bed," she said.

It had the ring of truth to it, Red decided as he looked out the window at the growing mass of people. Some of them were already tired of the sight and getting into their buggies or vehicles to go on back home. New ones arriving by the minute to take their places. More coming and going than he'd seen at the county fair. He could take anyone of the fools out in a moment. Didn't they have a lick of sense?

An automobile stopped in front of the old shed and a man in a three-piece suit looked out over the situation before he went inside. Tilly watched him carry out a wooden box right behind the sheriff and all the people. She could swear she saw him laugh as he drove away.

"Let Olivia go. You only need one hostage. If you keep both of us, us women will get to talking and the two of us can come with a plan to overthrow you. You know I will, Red. I'm bigger than you are and meaner too. I could whip your tail end when we were in the sixth grade and I still can." Tilly drew his attention from the window.

"You'd be my guarantee? You won't try to run if I let her go?" Red cocked his head to one side.

"Sure." Tilly nodded.

"I don't believe you. It's a trap. You got a gun hidin' on you somewhere? You going to get me to let her go and shoot me dead. That sheriff didn't even try very hard to stop you when you come runnin' in here."

"That idiot told me I couldn't come in here so I had to prove him wrong. I can outrun him any day of the week. Let Olivia go. She'll only drag you back and keep you from getting away." Tilly saw another wagon stop beside the shed. No one paid a bit of attention to it.

"Sheriff, we're trading hostages. I'm staying. Olivia is coming out," Tilly yelled through the window.

"Now, why'd you go and do that," Red shook his

head. "I didn't say I'd be willin' for that. Now you got
to make a liar out of me."

"You don't want to be a liar, do you, Red? Never
knew a Johnson to tell a lie. Drink some 'shine. Play
some cards. Do a little bar room fightin' but they don't
lie," Tilly said.

"He's a dirty monster," Olivia finally found her
voice. She shivered and put her hands over her face,
swollen from crying. "Please let me go," she sobbed.

"Oh, okay. I only need one of you and Tilly won't
give me near the trouble. 'Sides, I'd be a liar if I
didn't, even if Tilly said it and I didn't."

"Red, I want you to let both those women go,"
Ford's voice boomed through the heavy silence.

"Want in one hand. Spit in the other. See which one
fills up fastest," Red hollered back. "You can have this
whining one. I'll keep Tilly."

"I can go? You won't shoot me in the back?" Olivia
was already on her feet and headed toward the door.

"No, I ain't goin' to shoot you," Red said. "And I
don't lie."

Olivia ran out the door and into the sheriff's arms
where she proceeded to sob and almost faint. "He's
awful. He grabbed me by the hair and made me go
with him."

"Did he hurt you other than that?" Ford asked.

She shook her head. "He was drunk at first but now
he's sobering up and saying he's going to take the
money and go to Mexico."

"Is Tilly all right? Has he hurt her?" Ford asked,

fear gripping his heart. Great God in heaven above, he couldn't figure out why Tilly ran inside the house that way. If he'd had an inkling of an idea that she had such a thing on her mind, he would have handcuffed her to a tree. Did she think she was invincible? That a desperate robber wouldn't kill her if it would buy him freedom? The woman must think she could walk on water to voluntarily run into that house.

Tilly sat on the sofa and watched rigs and automobiles come and go in the excitement. None of them concerned her one bit. Them or Red Johnson. When the last of her customers took their merchandise and were gone, she'd deal with him.

"Now what?" Red asked.

"Now you tell them what you want and they give it to you, or else you kill me," she told him. Aha, there was the fourth automobile more interested in the shed than in the melee going on at Red's house.

"I want a car in the next hour. I want it full of gas and all them fool people off my property when it gets here. I'm takin' Tilly with me. I'll turn her loose at the first town I come to. Might be Ardmore or Wilson or somewhere else. But she'll get in touch with you when I do," he yelled out and fired another round off just to scare a few people into going home before he deftly reloaded the gun.

"We'll get it for you. Don't harm Tilly," Ford called back.

"Bet that hurt," she mumbled to herself. Down deep that lawman would like to pull the trigger on a shotgun aimed right at her heart.

"The fifth man who went inside the shed came out with his box covered in a toe sack. He walked toward the back of the cemetery and in a few minutes, Tilly saw the same man in a one-horse buggy leaving the area. That was all of them. Time to take matters into her own hands and go home.

She stood up and walked to the window where Red was busy keeping an eye out at the circus on the lawn. There was Nellie and Cornelia, who'd taken control of Olivia. She didn't see Bessie or Beulah, the other two women who lived at the Morning Glory, but she did spot Dulcie, their cook. Olivia was still slinging tears, milking the situation for all it was worth. There was Inez and George who owned the drugstore on Main Street, and half the rest of Healdton's population.

"Well, would you look at that?" she said. "I believe that's old Ben Slack out there. Look, Red. Over there by Maxine Holdman. She's liable to declare that he's got to make an honest woman out of her and marry her since he's standing close enough she can touch him."

Red began to chuckle. That changed rapidly to a loud laugh. When he threw his head back to guffaw, Tilly reached out and jerked the shotgun out of his hands.

"Now, why'd you do that?" Silence filled the room.

"Because we're going outside, Red. I'm not going to let you try to run and get killed. You'll do some time in the jail. Maybe a year, but you'll be alive when it's over. The money is all over there beside the settee and they'll recover it. Now you open the door and put your hands over your head."

"What if I say no, will you kill me?" he asked.

"Suppose so," Tilly told him.

"You wouldn't shoot old Red." He grinned.

"Want to try me?"

"You said you'd go with me. You said you'd be my hostage if I let that woman go," he whined.

"I lied."

"But . . ." he stammered as he raised his hands and laced his fingers behind his head.

"I said I never knew you to lie. I didn't say *I* wouldn't lie." She motioned for him to open the door and yelled through the window, "I'm bringing Red out. Don't shoot him or me. He's surrendering and y'all remember that when it comes time for the trial."

What had started out as a big problem ended rather anticlimactically when Ford met Red in the yard and slapped a pair of cuffs on his wrists, put him in the back of the sheriff's car and told everyone the spectacle was over.

"Why in the hell did you do that?" he growled as he took the shotgun from Tilly. "Do you even know how to shoot one of these? You did a foolish thing, Matilda Anderson. A very foolish thing."

"It got results and no one got killed in the process. You've got Red to keep you company in the jail for a long time and Olivia can claim the vapors for a week or more. And yes, sir, Mr. Lawman, I can shoot that thing. I can shoot the eyes out of a snake at twenty yards. So you'd better be sure you stay a little farther back than that when you're tailing me," she said. *And while y'all were paying attention to the fracas, I had a vantage point to keep an eye on my business in the shed,* she thought.

"You are crazy." He ran his fingers nervously through his jet-black hair.

"Been said before. I reckon it could be true," she told him as she climbed into her car and waved good-bye at half the town of Healdton. Tomorrow she'd put out fresh flowers on her Granny's grave and make a side trip into the old caretaker's shed.

Hopefully next week there wouldn't be a wedding or some other such thing at the church because that's where she'd told her buyers to find their next stash. At the far end of the path behind the church in the old outhouse that hadn't been used in more than a year. Not since Tucker got tired of running back there in the wintertime and put up the money to have a modern bathroom in the church house.

Chapter Five

Bessie and Beulah sat across the kitchen table from Tilly, both of them with frowns burrowed down in wrinkles produced after seventy years of living. From the stove, Dulcie, the cook and friend to the ladies, stirred a pot of boiling chicken. It smelled scrumptious. Evidently the ladies at Morning Glory were having dumplings for supper, one of Tilly's favorite meals.

"Well?" Bessie lowered her chin and gazed out over the top of her wire-rimmed spectacles.

"Can't do it?" Tilly shook her head.

"We ran that business with Katy for years. Took all three of us to deliver what she made in the basement under that barn. Made a good living for the bunch of us. Your mother learned the trade too. Pretty soon she'd helped Katy to double the outflow and we made even more. By the time that hurricane took her, you

68

were ready to learn. But there comes a time to quit and it's here, Matilda Jane. I never thought I'd tell you that, but you're about to get caught," Beulah said.

"That's the truth. Sheriff is smart," Dulcie put in her two cents. "He's one of them honest Indians too. Couldn't buy him if you tried. He won't turn his head and not see you out going to Ragtown or Hewitt on weekends. He knows what you're doing and one little slip will put you back in jail. I heard he's going to clean up the area and hire a local man for the sheriff and move on. That's the way he operates. At least shut down the stills until he's gone, Tilly."

"He'd win and I would lose. Makes me cranky when I lose." Tilly shook her head.

"You couldn't pass wind on Main Street without someone running to tell him what you ate for supper right now. Inez is watching you like a hawk. Overheard her whispering in the drugstore yesterday about how she thinks if they can break you, the other 'shiners will be scared into stopping. He goes in there every day at the same time and she makes sure she gives him all the gossip up to that point," Beulah said.

"Oh come on, darlin's. I know you all had your adversities when you were in the business. Ford Sloan just happens to be mine." Tilly stirred her lukewarm coffee.

"Baby girl, listen to us." Dulcie set a platter of oatmeal cookies on the table. "We're old but we can smell disaster and it's as thick in the air as the smell of this chicken broth."

Tilly ate three cookies while she thought about

what they were saying. True, two of them had been in business with her grandmother. One of them had known about it because she'd cooked for the Morning Glory for years and they were all three bosom buddies. But this was her call, not theirs.

"I'll be careful. I promise. If the heat gets too tough, I'll back off. Right now, I'm running it a little different. Last week, I about had heart failure when Red Johnson decided to up and rob the bank, but it worked out all right." She picked up another cookie and told them the story of why she'd really helped capture Red.

Bessie laughed until tears rolled down her wrinkled cheeks. Beulah got the hiccups and Dulcie shook her head until all three chins wobbled.

"I declare, girl. You could be Katy's daughter instead of her granddaughter." Dulcie pointed her finger right at Tilly. "But that was skinning the cat too close to the dogs. Where's the stash this week?"

"Can't tell you. You'd feel honor bound to help me and I can't have you going to the gallows too," Tilly teased. "Dulcie, I'm tucking a few more of these cookies into my purse. I'm off to the drugstore for a glass of lemonade."

"That's the lion's den," Bessie said. "Inez is the biggest gossip in the whole county and she's always fillin' the sheriff's head full when he goes in there for his coffee right before he has supper. She's been battin' her lashes at him like she wasn't a married woman. Don't know what the world is comin' to, I declare. George has been good to that woman. Nothing but a lion's den where you're concerned. You need to stay away from there."

"Know what tames a lion?" Tilly asked.

"What?" Dulcie asked.

"Fresh meat." Tilly giggled and hugged all three of them. "Libby will be by to keep you girls company tomorrow morning. Clara told me she was coming in to do some shopping. Libby loves you."

"Almost as much as you did at her age. Don't know what either one of us would have done when we lost our own kids if Katy hadn't been willin' to share you three with us." Bessie gave her another hug. "Be careful. And you let us know if you need help."

"I'll do it." Tilly waved good-bye at the kitchen door. The smile disappeared by the time she reached the front door. When she parked in front of the drugstore, her jaw ached from clenching her teeth. Damn that Inez, anyway. If she'd kept her business at home those three sweet ladies wouldn't be in a frenzy. She hated to see them upset and worried. Tarring Inez and rolling her in chicken feathers didn't seem like enough punishment. Maybe she should invite her to dinner, get her drunk on spiked tea, and put a bug in Ford's ear that she's the moonshiner in town.

"Well, good morning, Matilda," Inez said from behind the soda counter. "What on earth brings you to town in the middle of the week? Want a cold lemonade? Are you meeting Clara for some shopping?"

"No, darlin'." Tilly almost choked on the endearment but remembered what she'd told Ford. That she would call Tucker's ugliest mule darlin' and not to get any notions about it being a sweet nothing just for him. "I'm in town to meet a groom. You should charge admission to sit on your bench out front or spend time in here. It worked so well for Clara, don't you think? She sat on the bench out there for a decade before her real Prince Charming came along and carried her off. One day he did and she's been happy ever since. Ten years of coming in here every day wouldn't be too much of a price to pay for a good husband, I wouldn't think."

"You're teasing me." Inez put on a fake grin.

"Never know. I will have a lemonade while I wait. Clara didn't seem to mind the weather when she waited. Me, now, I think I'll just wait in here every day for the next ten years. Wind tears my hair all to pieces. What's been going on in town? Sheriff Sloan caught any moonshiners?"

"How would I know?" Inez's hands shook as she set the lemonade on the counter.

Tilly swiveled on the stool a bit before she took a long swig. The woman could make good lemonade. Not as good as Tucker's on a hot July day, but not bad. The clock hung high on the wall beside the bulletin board with the prices for lemonade, Coca-Cola, iced tea, coffee, and other sundry items. The time was exactly four twenty-eight. Tilly sipped her drink slowly for about two minutes. Just a little over a hundred seconds to make Inez uncomfortable.

"The preacher came by a while ago. Did you know his friend from Memphis is arriving today?" Inez talked fast in a high-pitched squeak.

"Nope, hadn't heard. Reckon he's my knight in shining armor? The one who'll drive up in a big white car or even a horse and carry me off to happy ever after?"

"I wouldn't know," Inez snapped. "The preacher said he just got the letter this morning and his friend is only going to be here from today until Sunday afternoon. So he's going to ask the friend to preach a little, short fall revival. Starting tomorrow instead of Wednesday night services, we're going to have a four-night revival, and the friend, I do believe his name is Johnny Jones. Yes, that's right, Jonathan Jones. He's going to preach the Sunday morning service. According to Julius, that's the proper procedure for visiting preacher friends. If he went to Memphis, he'd be expected to do the same. I do declare, that'll make a busy week for us, now won't it?"

"Four days. Better be love at first sight if he's my knight. Won't have time to get to know him very well like Clara had to get to know Briar. Oh, well, some of us aren't blessed like Clara, are we?"

Five more seconds. Four. Three. Two. One. The door opened and in walked none other than Sheriff Rayford Sloan himself. Just like Tilly planned. She'd think about the setback with the church revival later. At the time, she had other big-mouthed catfish to fry.

"Matilda." he nodded. "Inez, I'll have a cup of coffee. One sugar. No cream."

"I know," Inez said curtly and blushed.

"So did you come to be my knight in shining armor?" Tilly looked up at him, flirting blatantly.

Inez dropped the full cup of coffee on the floor, had to start all over again, and clean up the mess. She couldn't remember a time when she'd been so jittery, and of all days, the very one when she had news for the sheriff. She'd have to make a run down to the jail to deliver it, though, because it was about Tilly Anderson and she sure couldn't deliver it with the woman sitting right there beside the sheriff.

"Got butter on your fingers?" Tilly asked Inez.

"Just slipped," she said.

"What are you talking about? A knight in shining armor?" Ford swiveled his stool around to look directly at Tilly.

"Clara found one. I figure it has to be the power in this drugstore. It did take Clara ten years to get her knight, but surely if I come in here every day at the same time, I'll find mine and he'll carry me off to happy ever after." Tilly ran her tongue around her full lips to get the last drop of sweet lemonade.

"Sounds like a fool's errand to me." Ford turned back around to find his coffee sitting in front of him. "So what's new in town, Inez?"

"Not a thing." Inez sent him a long, sideways glance.

"Nothing about Red being in jail? I figured that would be the talk of the town after the way Tilly got him to come out and give up." Ford blew on the steaming coffee before he sipped.

"Folks do mention it sometimes." Inez rolled her eyes, hoping he'd understand that she couldn't talk with the very topic of the sizzling news she had sitting right there.

"Well, it was a crazy thing Tilly did, but at least no one was hurt," Ford said.

"You didn't really answer me, lawman? Are you my knight in shining armor or do you think it might be the new preacher who's coming to visit Julius. Think he might carry me away when he leaves Sunday afternoon?" Tilly asked.

"I'm not your knight, Tilly. Knights aren't allowed to carry off women of questionable character. Knights like innocent, sweet little things, but if the preacher has a hotline to heaven and can get you absolved of all your sins, he might be interested in donning his armor and shield and toting you away," the sheriff told her.

"Questionable character?" Tilly almost giggled but kept it under control.

"We both know what I'm talking about. Where's your stump?"

"Ain't got a stump. I got both legs and neither of them are fake. Want to see?"

Inez spewed iced tea in a fine spray all over the bulletin board in front of her. Ink ran in a long stream as the mist of tea stained the white paper showing the prices of everything. Crimson crawled from her neck all the way to her forehead and her big ears burned. She wanted to cover her face with her checked apron. She was afraid to turn around for fear she'd see Tilly jerking up her dress skirt to show her legs to the sheriff.

"You know very well what I'm talking about," Ford told her. "And no, I do not want to see your legs."

"Guess you really aren't my knight. He'd want to see if I had fake legs." Tilly kept on teasing.

"I'll find it, Tilly. I promise I will," he said.

"Are you daft? I have no idea what you're talking about. I did haul a couple of big stumps out of the pasture where Tucker had cut down trees for firewood. Is that what you're talking about? If it is, they're out behind my house and I intend to burn them. If you're crazy, talking in riddles the way you are, you aren't my knight. I'll have another glass of lemonade, please, Inez, when you get that tea cleaned off the counter. Guess it must have had bones in it, the way you choked on it."

Inez got control of her emotions and refilled Tilly's glass. "Sheriff, do you think barmy runs in families and if it does, can it be transferred from one member to the other when one is cured of it?" she said tartly.

"Wouldn't know. Who's barmy?" he answered.

"Well, Clara Anderson had a bit of it. A preacher man came through here in revival time and stayed at the Morning Glory. He and Clara fell in love and he promised to come back and get her in a week. Was going to pick her up right out in front of this drugstore and carry her away to marry her. Never did show up. Ten years she came every day at the same time and sat out there waiting for him. Wind. Rain. Sleet. Snow. Cold. Heat. Every single day. She seems to be cured since Briar Nelson married her, but I'm worried that Matilda may have gotten bit by it." She stared right at Tilly. The rich hussy wasn't going to intimidate her one bit.

"Don't think so." Ford chuckled. "This woman hasn't got a barmy notion. She's as conniving as a rattlesnake."

"Thank you, darlin'. But who's to say how crazy I might be. There's a new preacher in town and everyone knows history repeats itself. Maybe he'll make promises he can't keep and leave my poor little heart in shatters. That's when the real knight will sweep in and save me from being an old maid. Or maybe I'll kill him and plant his body under your lilac bush, Inez, and sit on the bench out front for ten years to throw everyone off the track." Tilly kept a grin at bay by looking at Inez. The woman would have to get up a whole lot earlier than she did to get ahead of Matilda Jane Anderson.

"Well, I've got work to do. Good day, ladies." Ford left the two cats to their own fight and escaped out the door.

Inez pouted. Now she'd have to go to the jail to tell him the gossip that there'd been interest in the old caretaker's shed at the cemetery the whole time Red held the bank's money and Olivia and Tilly as his hostages.

"Good day to you, lawman. But not good-bye because I've only just begun." Tilly raised the rest of her drink to his back in a salute.

"Matilda, you are shameless," Inez berated her.

"Been called that before. Keep the change." She tossed a quarter on the counter. "See you tomorrow, Inez." She left her car on the side of the street and followed Ford up the street. He went into the hotel.

So did she. He dragged up a chair and ordered supper. She chose a table right beside him and ordered the same thing.

"What are you doing, Tilly?" he asked.

"Same as you. Having supper," she answered, taking in the dim dining room in one glance. Six mismatched tables with an equal number of chairs around each. Thirty-six people could eat in this place at once. That meant the potential of a thousand meals served in a month at a dollar a plate. Bessie and Beulah should buy the hotel and sell the Morning Glory.

Unbleached, slightly stained muslin curtains covered the front window where a sign that advertised vacancies was propped up. Bare wood walls needed a coat of white paint to lighten up the room. The floor could use some of Clara's special wax to give it a shine. With a little work, it could invite people inside, rather than grab them and hold them down until they ordered.

She chanced a glance toward Ford, who glared at her. Well, that was too damn bad. He'd followed her everywhere the past couple of weeks. Now he could open up his sexy mouth and have a dose of his own medicine. His black eyes looked as if lightning bolts were going to start shooting from them at any minute. He sat as straight and stiff as a corpse but the muscles in his jaws gave proof that he was still alive. His full lips had firmed up into a thin line and she was sure if he tried to speak his voice would rival Inez's for squeak.

Her plate arrived. Meat loaf, mashed potatoes, string

beans, a biscuit, and a piece of cherry pie for dessert. Poor substitute vittles when she remembered Dulcie's dumplings, there for the sampling over at the Morning Glory. Out of her peripheral vision, she could see him frowning at his food. She hoped it soured on his stomach. She had better things to do than run around after him all evening, but she needed to know his routine. When did he do the evening check around town? When would he rattle the locks on the general store? When would he make sure everything was fine at the church?

Maybe she should give up the business. Seemed like a higher force was sure enough putting obstacles in her way. First the business with Red Johnson and the bank robbery and now the possibility of a revival, which would have people from all over the area coming to church on the very night her buyers would be coming around to visit the old outhouse. No, she would not! Ford Sloan wasn't going to win. She'd just have to outsmart him again. At least she had time to make a plan.

Ford made himself eat but felt no taste. He could have been putting hay and sawdust in his mouth. His sweet tea glass was refilled four times before he finished the last bite of beans. Normally, he wouldn't have eaten them anyway, since green beans were his least favorite vegetable. But he'd rather sit in an outhouse on a hot July day for six hours than let Matilda Anderson know she had the power to upset him.

Finally, he finished, wiped his mouth on the napkin and tossed it beside his plate. Trying to treat her as if she were nothing but a piece of furniture, he crossed the floor and, with a nod toward the clerk, left the hotel. He hadn't gone a dozen yards until he felt her behind him. He stopped at the general store and took in the window display. Inez, his gossip informant, might buy that garish-looking hat covered in flowers and fake birds but he couldn't imagine Tilly wearing such a monstrosity. She favored those little whiffs of nothing with a short veil that drove a man insane wondering if the beauty underneath it was as enticing as it appeared.

"I don't think that one suits your color. It's got too much green in it. It'd make you look a bit sallow," she whispered so close to him that the warmth of her breath traveled from shoulder-level to his ear.

"What are you doing?" he asked abruptly.

"I'm following you. Actually, I thought you'd be happy. After all, it makes it easy for you to keep tabs on me that way. You going to buy that hat?"

"You can stop now. I've got work to do today. I don't have time to shadow you," he said, staring at the hat, seeing her reflection in the window. For just a moment he wished she wasn't . . . he shook off the idea before it formed. He didn't need to even think such thoughts.

"Promise?" she asked.

"I'm on my way back to the jail for the rest of the evening. You running 'shine tonight?"

"Not tonight, darlin'. I do that on Friday nights. All but this next one. There's going to be a revival at church."

"Why do you even go to church?" he growled.

"Because I can't afford to have God mad at me," she said. "I'll be there on the back pew. Reckon you'll be out trying to put an end to wickedness in Carter County, won't you?"

"I'll be at that church right beside you and Tucker and Libby," he said between clenched teeth. "I don't believe you'll be there. You won't go two weeks without a delivery. You'll lose your customers."

"There're no stumps in the church," she told him.

"I wouldn't be surprised if you didn't have one under the altar. Besides, I know more than you think, Tilly. I'm telling you right now. Shut it down or I'll own it. All of it."

"Wouldn't know what you're talking about. You do have the strangest notions. Did a preacher promise to marry you and leave you at the altar? And here I thought you were a big, handsome man. Didn't know you had a thing for preachers? Does Julius know?"

Ford gritted his teeth. If homicide ever became legal, she was going to be the first woman he killed. "I do not have a thing for preachers."

"Whew!" She wiped her hand across her brow. "I thought maybe you were just a waste of good manhood."

"You are a brazen hussy," he said.

"And you are sitting beside one in church on Friday night, lawman. What's that say for your taste in women?"

"I'm going to the jail. Good day, Miss Anderson. You are exasperating, woman."

"Why, thank you. I believe that's the best compliment I've had in weeks. See you Friday night. I'm on my way to the cemetery to visit my Granny's grave site. Sure you don't want to follow me there?"

He threw up his hands and went around her toward the jail.

She followed him until she reached the drugstore where she'd parked her car. Checking the rearview mirror she made sure he really was going to the jail and drove toward the cemetery. It was the first time she'd had an opportunity to pick up her cash without a tail but she'd done an excellent job in making him angry enough he'd leave her alone the rest of the week.

She parked the car in front of the cemetery gates and walked inside. She meandered past the memorial spaces where her parents weren't buried. An elaborate stone there with their names, birth dates and death dates inscribed, stood beside her grandparents' graves. But there were no bodies below the earth. They'd never been recovered in what the sea had claimed during that hurricane. Granny had insisted on putting up a stone so Tilly would have a place to pay her respects so there it was. To their left stood a pink granite stone marking the place where her grandmother and grandfather had been laid to rest. To their right lay Tucker's parents and on down from them were Clara's. Spaces still remained in the wrought-iron enclosure for other members of the family when their lives ended.

"Granny, darlin', it's sure getting hard to keep on with the business. What would you tell me to do? Your old bosom buddies and sisters in crime think I should get out. Dulcie worries about me. Clara is scared to death. I keep thinking you'd laugh and give the lawman a run for his money," she mumbled as she touched the cold rock.

She stooped down and pulled a few weeds, checking the area for Ford as a precaution before she went to the shed. No one in sight. Not anywhere. She went straight to the shed and opened the door, barely hanging on one hinge. Sitting on a shelf with an old hoe and shovel leaned up against it, several bills waited under a rock. She shoved them in her pocket and turned to leave when the shadow passed in front of the window. Just as she picked up the hoe, Ford's frame filled the doorway.

"So I've found your stump. Where's the empty jars that Clara is going to can soup in tomorrow?" He folded his arms over his chest.

"No stumps here. Want to tear up the place looking for jars, have at it. I'm here to borrow a hoe to clean up around my Granny's grave. The caretaker has a new shed but he keeps it locked up all the time. I found an old rusty hoe in here, but I think it will chop weeds. Can't get them pulled with my hands."

Ford could've sworn he'd catch her with jars and money both. Inez had been waiting in his office with a tale about how Tilly's buyers had hoodwinked him right behind his back when he was trying to get Red Johnson to come out of the house last weekend. Looking down at her with a hoe in her hand, he began to wonder if Inez wasn't just spreading malicious gossip after all. And that Tilly was teasing him into believing that she was a moonshiner. He'd never been wrong before, but there was always a first time.

"You are a lucky woman." He moved to one side.

"You are a persistent man. Did Inez set the sidewalk on fire getting down to the jail? She's always had a thing for lawmen. Thinks she's helping them when she tells her tall tales. Watch what you believe, Ford. She'll have you dizzy from chasing your tail." Tilly went right past him, carrying the hoe in one hand and shoving the other deep into her pocket to keep a roll of bills secure.

He checked the shed out of curiosity more than anything. He found a shovel and little else. Not even a single jar, empty or full. No money. No booze. Nothing. Who, exactly was telling the truth and who was jerking his chain? Tilly was hoeing inside a white cast-iron fence when he rode his big black stallion out of the graveyard.

Chapter Six

The moon was high in the sky, daylight still a couple of hours away when Tilly arose that Friday morning. She slipped into her overalls and flannel shirt, scrounged around until she found a jacket to keep out the fall nip in the air, and tugged on her work boots. She sipped cold coffee from a cup she'd left on the counter the night before. It took the morning taste out of her mouth, even if it couldn't do any better job of removing the horrid taste left in her heart from the revival the night before.

Julius had introduced his friend, Johnathan Jones, to her on Wednesday night before the services. A tall, handsome man with light hair and brown eyes. Just the right amount of angles to his face to make him handsome. A thin, mean mouth though that didn't invite kisses. On Thursday night he'd preached for an hour and a half, even more dramatic than Julius, on the evils of drink. Not only the moonshine makers and runners were swinging by a thread the size of a spiderweb over hell's gaping mouth, but he advocated total abstinence for everyone. Even in times of deepest sickness, the Lord and Savior would not forgive a person who had a shot of whiskey to keep him from coughing up his toenails. Why, even smelling it would guarantee a front row seat right in hell.

After the last hymn was sung she was on her way out when Johnny caught her in the yard and asked her opinion on his sermon. The heated argument lasted fifteen minutes and left her in a bad mood. The man was radical with a capital R, and she had no intentions of going back to listen to him again. However, she wasn't quite sure how to keep an eye on her business if she didn't.

She drew the jacket closer to her chest as she made her way to the barn in the dark. Without lighting a lantern she moved a few bales of hay and opened the basement door. All the familiar smells met her as she found her way down the steps, not needing to see but knowing from years of experience where everything was. She picked up the first box of twelve jars and carried them back up and put them in the back of her car. Several trips later she reset the hay bales, locked the doors of the barn, and went to deliver her goods.

Not a soul in sight as she stacked all the boxes in the old outhouse right between the two holes. Underneath the jars was a simple note that told the buyers where the next drop-off would be. This time though, she'd have to figure out a way to get back into the old outhouse on Saturday morning before the services that night. It wasn't a common occurrence, but occasionally someone did make a fast run to the outhouse when the new modern one was occupied, and she couldn't have some little four-year-old finding her money. She'd just have to pick it up before or during Saturday night services. Poor little Johnny Jones would have need of the outhouse if he knew what was sitting between those two holes.

By the time she got back to her house a brilliant sunrise met her. Brilliant orange. Lemon yellow. A touch of pink laced here and there. She sat on the back porch and tried to let the beauty sink into her soul. It didn't work. All she could think about was the way that preacher had looked down on her, telling her that she was a beautiful woman but with her brazenness she'd be an old maid. No man would ever want a woman who'd stand up to a preacher and tell him he was wrong.

"Well, you got that right," she had said. "Especially if it's a preacher who wants me. It don't matter if it's a preacher who's interested in me or the town drunk, I will speak my mind, especially when I'm asked for my opinion. And darlin', any man is not better than no man. I've lived without your kind for nigh onto thirty years. I expect my heart won't stop beating if I don't have one for the next thirty."

She remembered the words and wished she'd thrown in a few "damns" and "hells bells" to make him even angrier. As if her grandmother were standing behind her, she heard the familiar words: "Matilda

Jane, if you are upset, good hard work will take it out of you."

"Okay, okay," Tilly muttered. "The hardest work in the world is housework so let's go wash that man's vision out of my mind. But you'd better be right, Granny. If I clean a room and can still see his sneer when I argued with him I'm going to pitch a hissy fit. Evidently the women in his world all walk six steps behind their man and only unzip their lips to ask what they want for supper."

She made pancakes for breakfast and a fresh pot of coffee, black as tar and stronger than steel. While she ate, she took stock of the kitchen. Dirty dishes from two days before, grease on the side of the stove, and the refrigerator had things growing in it that could begin to breathe any day if she didn't clean it out. She rolled up her sleeves and attacked it. At noon the whole place was shiny clean, rivaling Dulcie's kitchen at the Morning Glory, and almost as spotless as Clara's. She leaned on the doorjamb and stared at it, and right there in the middle of the kitchen floor was a vision of Reverend Johnny Jones.

"More work. I haven't worked that fool out of my mind," she whispered and turned around to look at the dining room. Dust an inch thick on the chair rungs, table piled a foot high with newspapers and magazines. Dirty windows. Stained curtains.

"Why couldn't something other than hard work erase anger?" she whined. She grabbed a ribbon from the top of the pile of paper on the table and tied her hair back. First things first. Start up the new Upton washing machine. It had been the best investment she'd made the previous year. As bad as she hated laundry day, it did prevent her from leaving all her delicate things in the hands of the commercial laundry in Healdton. She filled the tank with water, plugged it in and added soap.

While it agitated she took the curtains down and shoved them down into the water, then went back to the dining room to clean the windows. With sunlight streaming through the dingy windows she could really see the dust and clutter. It took two hours to get it livable and the burning barrel in the backyard was full to the brim. She'd burn it later, when curtains weren't flapping on the clothesline in the warm afternoon sun.

She stood in the doorway, eyeing the dining room that hadn't had a cleaning like that in at least five years according to the dates on some of the magazines and newspapers. When she turned around there was the good reverend's apparition sneering at her from right beside the Victrola.

"He'd probably disagree with music and dancing too. Maybe that's the hell fire and damnation sermon he'll preach tonight." She didn't even look around but began taking down the curtains in that room. She'd work until she was so tired she would fall into bed and there would be nothing in her mind. Not even the handsome sheriff and his badge to threaten her.

At dusk she had the curtains back on the windows and, true to her grandmother's words, she was tired enough that all she could see when she shut her eyes was a feather bed calling her name. She scrambled a half dozen eggs and fried a dozen slices of bacon, made toast, and devoured the whole plate of food while standing beside the sink. When she finished she carefully cleaned up the mess and vowed she'd never let things get in such a horrid mess again.

She ran a bath and dropped her dirty clothing on the floor beside the tub, promising that she'd pick them up as soon as she finished soaking. Leaning back in the deep, warm water, her stomach filled, her anger sated, she dozed. When she awoke the water was chilly, she had goose bumps the size of the Arbuckle Mountains, and she had a second wind.

"And I'm not using it to go to church or to clean the upstairs," she declared, wrapping a big towel around her when she stepped out of the tub. "It'll take another mad attack to get this part of the house in order. Maybe that won't happen for another five years. Lord, but I hate to clean."

She was about to slip into a nightgown when she heard the roar of a car and saw headlights coming up her lane. She hurriedly pulled on drawers, threw a slip over her head and a faded blue cotton dress. It had to be Clara because she was the only one, other than Tucker, who came uninvited, and after dark it meant something was wrong. Tilly didn't bother with stockings or shoes. She ran down the stairs and threw open the front door just as Ford reached up to knock on it.

His mouth went dry at the sight of her on the other side of the screen door. Barefoot. Faded dress. Damp hair falling to her hips. He hadn't even expected her to be home, but figured she'd be out at her stump. When she didn't show up at church, he'd left to drive through the cemetery. Nothing there. He was sure she'd found another place to make the delivery and she'd duped him into believing she would be in church so he'd go there. He was angry when the caretaker's shed didn't have a thing in it and decided to drive out to her place just to see if she was home or out making a run. What was barely a foot from him with only a sheet of screen wire keeping his lips from hers set his heart to beating double-time.

"Is something wrong? Is Clara all right? Tucker?" Her voice carried worry.

He couldn't remember when a woman had been concerned about him. It must be nice. "Everything is fine, I would suppose. Truthfully, I didn't expect you to be home. I thought someone in your profession would be out taking care of business."

"I don't plow or feed cattle at night, Mr. Sloan," she said.

"Then I'll be on my way." He tipped his hat.

"No need to get in a rush. Come in and I'll make a pitcher of tea or a pot of coffee." If she could keep him occupied a couple of hours, her supplies would be picked up without a hitch. Maybe she'd been wrong when she'd thought everything was going wrong. Nothing could be better. Except that she had on her oldest dress, was barefoot, her hair was a wet mess and even with a bit of a second wind, she was tired enough that she'd have to fight to stay awake.

"Are you sure you're not busy?" he asked, reluctant to leave but afraid to stay.

"Been busy all day." She opened the screen and stood aside for him to come inside. "Had a mad on that I had to work off. That's the medicine Granny prescribed when I was in a snit, so I took a dose."

"Thought you didn't clean." He laid his hat on the foyer table and gazed into the living room. "Looks pretty decent to me." He noticed a Victrola and a library table with records scattered on the top. The sofa was inviting with its big round velvet arms and deep cushions.

"Cleaning is the curing medicine. I hate it worse than castor oil or Black Draught. But it works. I'm not angry anymore." She motioned him into the living room. "Have a seat. So you went to church? Did the good reverend start out with how dangerous it is to enjoy life?"

"That who you're mad at? I heard the two of you got into a pretty good discussion on the church lawn last night," he said. The cushions were soft and the arms just the right height. A man could do a lot of thinking on a sofa like this.

"That's who I was mad at. I'm not anymore. Don't have enough energy for anger. Want to go with me into the kitchen and make sure I don't have a still operating on the back of the stove? I'll make a pitcher of iced tea. Don't have any cookies or cake to offer you. Don't bake very often."

"No, I think I'll sit right here and enjoy being in a real house and a real living room all alone," he told her.

She left him with his head leaned back and his eyes shut. She wondered what exactly was in those two rooms above the jail. Surely they had a comfortable sofa for him to sit on while he read. Or maybe he had a Victrola up there and enjoyed music. She grinned as she lit the burner on top of the stove and put water on to boil, tea leaves into a crock pitcher and sugar cubes into a crystal bowl. She tiptoed across the dining room and peeped into the living room twice while she waited on the tea to steep. Both times he hadn't moved a muscle.

Ford heard her moving around in the kitchen, was aware of both times she padded back and forth and peered in at him, but he never opened his eyes. He didn't care if she took three hours to make tea; if she ranted and raved about the preacher all night. Just to sit still in a house with a woman in a cotton dress and her hair down was enough to pay for all of it. Even if it was Matilda Jane Anderson, his sworn enemy.

"What you got over there?" He tilted his head toward the Victrola when she brought the pitcher of tea and two glasses on a tray.

"I like modern music. Got some of the Original Dixieland Jazz Band, Nora Bayes, and Al Jolson. You want to listen to something?" She poured the tea.

He picked up a glass. Exactly right. The proper color and sweet. He guzzled all of it and refilled his glass. "I would love to listen to music. Anything you have. It's been a long time since I've been in a place that had a Victrola."

She put on "Shine On, Harvest Moon" by Nora Bayes and sat down on the far end of the sofa to listen, crossing her legs and keeping time with her foot to the music. When that ended, she let him hear the newest thing she'd bought in Ardmore just the week before, "Livery Stable Blues," by the Original Dixieland Jazz Band.

"Haven't heard that." He felt himself loosening up. "I like it. Like the sound. It would be a good dance tune."

"You dance?" she asked incredulously.

"Haven't in a while but I do like to dance. When I was a teenager I didn't miss a single barn dance. Had my eye set on a blond, blue-eyed beauty from the next farm over. She didn't know I was alive so I never got to dance with her but I did manage to dance with a lot of the other girls."

"Why?"

"Because they were willing."

"No, why didn't she know you were alive?"

"I'm a quarter Indian, Tilly. Blond, blue-eyed beauties didn't look at me and if she had, her mother and father would have thrown a fit. Probably sent her off to Boston or New York to some kind of boarding school."

"I'm a quarter Indian, Ford. I don't use it as a crutch. I go after what I want," she told him.

"No, you aren't. You've got blue eyes." He sat up straighter and studied her seriously.

"Got them from my mother. Granny Anderson was named Katy Evening Star Hawk. She was full-blood Indian. She's why Tucker's mother named the ranch that, remember? We told that story when you were there."

"But I didn't know she was Indian," he protested. Yes, the cheekbones were there. Delicate, but still visible. "Your mother had blue eyes?"

"Yes, she did. So did Tucker's and Clara's. Strange how we all got that and the dark hair from the Indian side. But why didn't you just walk up to Miss Beautiful Blond and ask her to dance? If I wanted to dance with a guy, I found a way to get him to ask me."

"I was thirteen." He chuckled. "The rejection factor is pretty strong at that age. By the time I was fourteen she'd moved away."

"Were you trying to make me feel sorry for you and swoon over the fact you've got Indian blood? Is that the way you get women to flock to you like flies to a fresh cow patty?"

"Works sometimes. I get a few dances that way." He grinned as he stood up, went over to the Victrola and picked out a record and carefully put it on to play. A slow song, "Wait Until Tomorrow," filled the room, but not as much as his presence when he crossed the room and held out his hand to Tilly. "Could I have this dance, please, ma'am? I've been looking at your pretty blue eyes from across the room all night."

"Of course." She nodded.

The touch of his hand engulfing hers sent delicious shivers down her arms and a warm tingling feeling in her heart. The feel of him close to her as they began the Foxtrot, a dance written to music set in 4/4 time when the couple moves in small fluid movements. She was amazed at how a man as big as Ford could get around the living room floor with such grace. He didn't miss a step and he spent the whole song looking down into her eyes.

She couldn't have looked away if she'd had the choice of doing so or being shot at sunrise. Neither could he. How could a woman totally mesmerize him so? He wondered as he kept time to the music. She was as light as a feather on her feet, didn't stumble even once. He'd never danced with a woman with such expertise before. And he didn't intend to stop with one dance either.

When the music stopped he bowed elegantly, thanked her for the privilege, and went to the record player to put another tune on. He carefully picked up the needle and set it down at just the right spot and went back to the sofa where she was curled up in the corner. "Another, ma'am? I fear the other ladies with blue eyes don't dance with Indian men."

"My pleasure." She reached for his hand. The jolt almost glued her to the floor. "This sure beats listening to the preacher." She looked up into his eyes again.

"I think he was about to start on the dangers of new modern dances. He'd mentioned the Hesitation Waltz and was into the Maple Leaf Rag as I walked out the back door. Declared that a man and woman were asking for the fire from hell to come right up and lick their toes if they were caught doing something like dancing." Ford's voice was husky.

"I knew it! I really did. I figured he'd do a night on the evils of liquor, one on dancing, one on adultery, and Sunday he'll preach on the forgiveness of God and ask for new converts," she said.

"Sounds about right. So tomorrow night will be adultery. Are you married?"

"Good Lord, no!" she exclaimed.

"Shucks. I got an idea you really do run 'shine. Tonight he's singeing our hair because we dance. I thought if you were married, we could blow the bottom out of his whole revival and repent on Sunday morning," he teased.

"Mr. Sloan, you are incorrigible. Are you suggesting that you would commit adultery?"

"Of course not." He laughed. "I wouldn't want to be on the run for the rest of my life from some woman's husband. It was just a joke." But was it? He questioned himself. Would he like to do more with Tilly Anderson than just dance in her living room?

She leaned her head on his chest, surprised to hear his heart beating just a little too fast, liking the feel of his muscles even through the chambray shirt and vest. This was the kind of man she wanted to spend the rest of her life with. Too bad he had to be a lawman. She might even overlook that with his ability to dance and willingness to do so. At least for a moment she thought so, but it didn't take long for her tired mind to realize what that kind of thinking would cost her. One night of unchaperoned dancing was all she could afford. She fully well intended to keep him there as long as she could so her clients could pick up their supplies. But she'd have to be very careful not to let him in her house again. Temptation was just too strong when she was in his arms. There wasn't enough repenting on Sunday to take care of the feelings she was battling. Too bad she'd had to work off a hissy that day. If he'd seen things before they were cleaned, he'd have run like a scalded hound and she wouldn't have to worry about him ever knocking on her door again.

Ford never thought he'd be dancing with Tilly. Especially in her house. Her, with no shoes. Him, without a chip on his shoulder concerning his heritage. Freedom, with a woman in a worn cotton dress and a Victrola. For the first time in his life there was a yearning in his heart for more than what would fit in the roll-top trunk in his two rooms above the jail. A wife. A farm. A child like Libby.

The music ended. This time she did a perfect curtsy and thanked him for the dance. "Now let's sit and visit awhile."

"Wear you out, did I?" He sat down on the opposite end of the sofa and watched her take the other end. She sat on her feet and draped her dress tail over her naked toes. He wished she would have crossed her legs again so he could see her feet and watch her keep time to the music. He'd never been around a woman who was so comfortable with herself.

"Yep, plumb out. Remember, I worked like a dog all day getting my pig pen mucked out," she told him. "What did you do today, other than play checkers with Red?"

"Not much. Pretty quiet in town. No murders. Not even over in Wirt. No fistfights. But that could all change by tomorrow night. Saturday night, men folks have their week's paycheck or else they just come to town for a change of pace. That's when I begin to earn my paycheck."

"You like what you do?" She looked at the star pinned on his denim vest.

"Sure. It's all I've ever known so I guess I like it. Might as well. To not like it would make a miserable day."

"If you could do anything in the world, what would it be?"

"You first," he said.

"I'd do just what I do now. I love the land. Love farming and cattle. Only difference is I'd want Clara to give me Libby," she said honestly.

"Why on earth would you want that?"

"Because I want a daughter and the conventional way to get one isn't socially acceptable," she said honestly, not remembering when she'd ever been comfortable enough to talk to a man like she was doing.

"Oh? I thought it was all right to have a family. Your knight in shining armor might not be the preacher, but he will come along some day, Tilly, and you can have your own daughter," he told her.

"Nope, I meant without a husband. Just a tomcat father."

"A what?" He looked at her like she was crazy.

"A tomcat father. You know a tomcat impregnates the female cat, and he goes on his merry way. She has the kittens and raises them all alone."

"Good Lord!" A whoosh left his lungs.

"See. Socially unacceptable."

"Amen, sister. To be talking like that to a man right now is even socially wrong. The preacher would have us hung up by the heels over hell's flames for dancing and having this conversation."

"I feel the heat already." She had to smile at the vision of the two of them being upside down, their bodies swinging so close that she could steal a kiss from him.

"What about you now? Got any dark secrets about your goals that the good traveling preacher would condemn you for?" she asked, hoping he couldn't see the blush setting her face on fire.

"Well, I'm not looking for a tomcat kid," he said with a wide grin showing off even white teeth. "But I suppose if I ever do settle down it'll be on a farm like this. Reminds me of the one I grew up on. Or my Grandfather Sloan's place over in Arkansas. We went there one time and I really liked it. Probably, looking back, it wasn't the farm but the feeling I had that summer. Like I belonged. I was an Irishman. Sixteen years old. Worked like a plow mule all summer helping him, and would have stayed forever listening to his wild tales about the Irish faeries and folklore."

"Think you will? Settle down?"

"No. I've got a trunk in my room. It takes about fifteen minutes to pack it and be ready to leave any town. Got a rule I live by. Nothing that won't fit in that trunk goes with me." He didn't look at her but at the empty glass of tea on the table in front of him. "Guess it's time for me to go now. Church will be letting out and Red will be looking for his last checker game of the day before we turn out the lights."

"I've enjoyed your company." She walked him to the door.

"Really? Did you really?" he asked.

"Yes, I did," she admitted.

He turned abruptly to tell her that he'd enjoyed the dances and the conversation, as unorthodox and crazy as it was. When he did she ran right into his chest. He looked down and she looked up. Sparks encircled them like a ring of fire with old Indians doing a pow-wow chant around the flames. Their lips met some-where in between him bending down and her tiptoeing. Warmth oozed down into their souls and tied a firm knot around both of their hearts.

"Good night, Matilda Jane." he finally drew away and picked up his hat from the foyer table. "I ought to apologize for that, I suppose, but I can't."

"Why apologize? I wanted it as bad as you did. But don't think it's the first of many. It's the last of one, lawman. It wouldn't work." She crossed her arms and hugged herself to keep from running into his arms and begging for another kiss.

"You got that right, lady," he agreed.

"See you in church Sunday?" She walked out onto the porch into the cool night air, not wanting him to go, yet wishing he was already gone.

"Wouldn't miss it. You got moonshine hid under the altar? Are the deacons going to leave you money there right after services?" he asked, reminding himself to keep their relationship where it belonged. Business. As in him putting her out of it.

"Sure I do," she told him. "Check the deacons' houses tomorrow night. They'll all be drunk as skunks. And if you believe that, darlin', you better pack up that trunk and get the hell out of Healdton."

Chapter Seven

Red Johnson shoved his thin arm out between the bars of the jail and moved a black checker, topped it off with a king and waited for Ford's move. His eyes were clearer than they'd been in months. His faded overalls and threadbare flannel shirt were clean and his hands weren't shaking anymore. Two weeks behind bars, with no liquor, had been pure hell. First he'd sweated and seen spiders on the ceiling. Before long, bugs were crawling on his skin and he'd yelled at Ford to kill them. But the last four days he'd had a clear mind and steady hands. The hours and hours he'd had time to think had produced a quiet man of few words.

"Looks like you got me cornered again." Ford's mind was not on the game.

"Yep."

"Red, you know Matilda Anderson pretty good don't you?"

"Yep."

"What do you know about her?"

"She's pretty."

"That's all?" Ford raised a dark eyebrow and made a move that lost him the game.

"Smart."

"Inez comes in here telling me about her being a moonshiner and all these stories about her grand-mother. She declares that Tilly is running 'shine even today. Says she's changing her delivery spots. That it was at the cemetery the night we brought you in and at the church the next week. Swears that Tilly went to the outhouse when the bathroom was empty during ser-vices and she could have used the one inside. No one does that, according to Inez. Says that it's smelly for one thing. And that there was talk of an unusual amount of activity around the church on Friday night. Could have just been young people looking for a place to be alone, but it might have been buyers picking up their stock. I don't know if Tilly is innocent and mak-ing me chase my tail because she's angry or if she's guilty."

Red grinned, something he hadn't done in weeks, showing tobacco stained teeth. "What does it matter?"

"I went out there last week. Thought she'd skipped out on church. I'd said earlier in the week I'd be right there beside her on the back pew so I could keep an eye on her. I try to aggravate her so bad she makes a slip up. I swore I'd own that car of hers before I left town. Since I was at church and she knew I'd be there, it would have been a perfect time for her to make her own deliveries. I knocked on the door and there she was all clean and fresh after a bath. Been cleaning house all day."

"Tilly, cleaning?"

"Guess it was a history-making event." Ford shook his head. "She was wearing a faded blue cotton dress and barefoot."

"Tilly?"

"She invited me in for iced tea. Now would she do that if she had plans to be out running moonshine? I don't think so. She put on some of her music and danced two times with me right there in the living room."

"Put on any shoes?"

"No, and she's a good dancer. She made tea and we talked about things that would scald the preacher's ears. Not improper things. Wouldn't want you to think that kind of thing. But she's very modern and outspoken."

"Yep."

"She always been like that?" Ford put the checkerboard away and leaned on the back two legs of the chair, propping his feet on the cell bars.

"Yep."

"You grew up with her, right?"

"Yep."

"You think she's running 'shine?"

"Maybe. Maybe not."

"What's that mean?" Ford asked.

"What does it matter?" Red had long since gotten over his anger at Tilly for hoodwinking him into giving himself up. After he'd studied the situation, he'd come to the conclusion that she'd saved his neck. Quite literally.

"What do you mean?" Ford cocked his head to one side. "It matters. If she's making and running 'shine out there on that farm, it's my business to put an end to it."

"Why? She ain't hurtin' nobody if she is." Red squinted. That sure wasn't the lantern putting that glow on the sheriff's face. Holy smoke! The man had been moonstruck and by none other than Miss Matilda Jane Anderson. Well, he damn sure wasn't the first and if he was the last, there'd be a snow in July right in Healdton, Oklahoma. Or a flood, ending this blasted ten-year drought. Since Tilly turned thirteen, there'd been boys standing in line just to get a chance to share a moment of space and time with her. A few had made it to the first date. He didn't know of a single one that got to the second one.

"Yes, she is." The chair sounded like a shotgun blast when the front two legs hit the wooden floor. "She's breaking the law if she's doing something illegal."

"Guess so." Red yawned.

"You wouldn't tell me if she was, would you?"

"Nope." Red moved over to the cot and sat down, took off his shoes and shoved them back under the narrow bed.

"Why would you protect her? She took your shotgun and marched you out of the house. If she hadn't run in there, you might have gotten away with that money. You had a hostage and we were looking for a car so you could get out of town. So tell me why you won't rat her out or at least defend her?"

"Tilly don't need nobody to protect her. She's tough. Saved my life." Red stretched out on the bed and folded his hands over his chest. "Be sober in a year. Can start all over."

"Who do I believe? Inez tells me stuff. Tilly won't give me any satisfaction about any of it."

"Cut Inez's tongue out. Good night, Sheriff." Red shut his eyes.

Ford checked his pocket watch. Nine o'clock. Things should be heated up really good in Wirt—Ragtown, as the locals still called it—by this time. He probably needed to drive out that way and make his presence known. From what he'd heard the town wasn't anything like it had been at the very first of the boom, but still it needed lots of work. At least the tents were disappearing and company houses standing in their place. Rental property for the oil men with families. Bring in the wives and it didn't take nearly so long to make a respectable place out of a boomtown. They brought children and wanted churches and schools. They hated brothels and saloons and kept a tight reign on their men folks. Sure made his job a lot easier when the wives and kids came to town.

He thought about Tilly as he drove toward Wirt. Memories of the sight of her barefoot and in that faded blue dress were engraved on his brain as if it had been branded there with a hot iron. Thinking about how she'd fit in his arms engulfed his heart, warming his whole chest. The aura surrounding her as she sat on the end of the sofa with her feet drawn up under her set well in his lonely soul.

Tilly was glad the sheriff had stopped scaring the bejesus out of her every time she turned a corner. Since that night of the infamous kiss, as she'd come to think of it when she had time to analyze the flames in her heart, he'd kept his distance. Didn't even sit beside her on the back pew in church. She'd driven right past the jailhouse and waved at him the previous night. The back end of the Sweet Tilly had been filled with five boxes of 'shine. Sweat poured out of her pores in spite of the cool night air. She'd never figured on him being outside the jailhouse, sitting in a chair, reading a book by the light coming through the window behind him. She surely would have made a wide circle around town if she'd even had an inkling of an idea that he'd be within ten feet of the Sweet Tilly all loaded up with moonshine. Nervously, she'd watched in the rearview until she turned off the rutted road into a grassy lane leading up to an old windmill. That's where she'd told her buyers they could find their product that night, but not to come for it until midnight. She almost swore off the business as she unloaded the boxes and kept a close eye out for a big looming shadow that certainly wasn't going to ask her to dance with him.

On Saturday she'd worked the second floor of her house over just to get rid of the jitters and tried to make up her mind to do what Clara and the ladies at the Morning Glory had wanted begged her to do . . . shut down the business. But she couldn't. Those stills could easily be the longest running in the whole nation. They'd been started when her Granny was a little girl. Good copper tanks that would cost a small fortune these days. But they'd paid for themselves time and time again. These days Tilly had her hands in lots of enterprises that brought in money but every time she went down in the basement to start a new mash or distill off a fresh batch, she remembered all the good times she'd had with her grandmother. All the things they'd talked about and the advice Katy had given her while they worked on the moonshine. The stories Katy had told about the times she'd nearly gotten caught or the night she finally got up enough nerve to tell her husband where their extra money was coming from.

Tilly had finished dusting and cleaning the entire upper floor of the house by suppertime but she still hadn't convinced herself that she should give up her business. Even if it was the one that brought in the least profit of all her ventures. She took a bath and put on her overalls and flannel shirt. No, that wouldn't work at all, she decided as she took them off and chose a dress from her closet. If she was stopped, at least she could make up a plausible story. There was no way Ford would believe she'd been to see a friend dressed in her boy clothing. It was just after eight thirty and fully dark when she backed the Sweet Tilly out and drove down the lane.

She drove cautiously to the windmill and picked up

her money. She shoved it down into her dress pocket and jumped when a raccoon ran past her feet, shuffling through the dry leaves. She'd never had jitters before and for that she could strangle Sheriff Rayford Sloan. That and the fact that she was losing jars every week now. She sure couldn't take a chance on taking empties back to the house with His Royal Sheriff Highness stuck to her like wallpaper glue. Seemed a small price to pay, but one of the things Granny Katy had told her in the beginning of the tutoring was to bring your jars home. Yes, they were expensive to replace but that wasn't the reason. If a woman started buying jars every spring and yet never canning a thing, talk would get around fast that she was doing something with quart jars. Something like moonshine running. Maybe when all the jars in the cellar were gone, and the ones down in the basement and those on the attic were used up, she might have to reevaluate the decision of giving up the business.

Still expecting to find him lurking about in the shadows, she started up her car and, without turning on the headlights, made her way to the main road by the light of the moon. She'd no more than turned back to the east, toward Healdton, when she saw a man walking along the road in long strides. It wasn't unusual to see people walking the three miles from Wirt to Healdton and back. Oil men going to court good girls over in Healdton; local men folks going to visit the brothels or the wild and wooly bars in Wirt. There'd be a time when Wirt was as clean as Healdton. When it had a hotel that only served illegal liquor to certain patrons in the back room the sheriff didn't know about. When it had several churches where the folks could go pray for a crop failure after they'd sowed their wild oats on Saturday night. But right now, Wirt was still a boomtown and barely made an effort to cover up the liquor and women.

She passed the man before she realized the gait and the slope of the shoulders belonged to Julius, the preacher of her church. She stomped on the brakes, creating a cloud of dust floating up from the rutted dirt road to drift through the windows and settle on everything around her. She coughed and swatted at the dust, leaning out the window to look back. Like an apparition, the preacher came through the dust fog with a big smile on his face.

"Evenin', Miss Tilly. I thought that was you and was hoping you'd stop. Could I beg a ride back to the parsonage?" Without waiting for an answer he trotted around the front of the vehicle and opened the passenger door.

"What on earth are you doing out at this time of the night?" she asked.

He crawled inside and shut the door. "Ladies in Wirt are trying to get up enough interest amongst the folks to put up a church building. Since they don't have a place to worship and it's a bit far for ladies with children to walk three miles to church on Sunday, I agreed to go over there on Friday night and preach a little for them," he explained.

"Where?" she asked.

"Oh, they've pitched a tent right across from Lucky's," he said seriously.

She commenced to drive, trying not to giggle. Lucky was the very man who ran a pool hall, drinking on the sly, and girls if you want business. He was one of her regular customers. She couldn't imagine a church service right across the street from that. Bawdy women on one side of the street. Certifiable saints on the other. Dixieland jazz and hymns meeting up in the middle of the street in a battle to see which could be the loudest. Menfolks sitting in body beside their wives and children; their spirits across the street playing poker and listening to a fast piano.

"Figure if we can make those men uncomfortable enough they'll join our side and give their hearts to the lord," Julius said.

"And if the tent is right across the street, the women can see if their husbands are being lead astray by Lucky. If they say they're working late at the oil wells, they'd better be there and not at Lucky's," Tilly said.

"Exactly right. The ladies have put aside enough money to buy that lot where the tent is and that's where we're going to build the church. At first, if they can't find a preacher, I've given my word that I'll come over on Sunday afternoon for services and we'll have a Bible study on Fridays. Tonight was our first service. Had a good turnout."

"That's nice." Tilly nodded.

"Tilly, I know you had words with my friend a couple of weeks ago. I know what the gossip is in town about you running moonshine. I know the sheriff is trying to catch you and has made his brag about owning the Sweet Tilly. If you are doing those things on the sly, I have to tell you . . ."

Before he could deliver a private sermon from a passenger seat soap box, approaching headlights caused Tilly to slow down and pull as far as she could over to the side to let the other car pass.

Ford's lights lit up the metal plate on the front of Tilly's car, showing him the Sweet Tilly was on the road that night, coming from Wirt and there were two silhouettes in the automobile. He slowed down and tried to peek inside to see just who was out traveling with Tilly at that time of the night, but all he could see was a head. It could be a man or it could be a woman with her hair slicked back. He passed the car and at the next available wide place in the road, turned around and went back.

He shot around the car about a mile from where he'd first seen her and stopped in the middle of the road. As sheriff, he had the right to stop anyone he thought might be in the moonshine business. As the man who'd kissed her, he wanted to know exactly who was riding with her whether it was his business or not.

Tilly came to an abrupt halt and waited for Ford to slowly saunter through the dust to her side of the car. He leaned down and peered inside, letting his eyes sweep over her into the back, checking for anything suspicious. "Evening, folks. What are you two doing out this late?"

"Coming from church services over in Wirt, Sheriff," Julius piped right up. "Miss Tilly was good enough to give me a ride back home."

"What were you doing in Wirt?" He gazed into her eyes, a dark steely blue in the dim moonlight.

"I would think, sir, that's none of your business," she retorted.

"Did you accompany Julius to church?" He ignored her sarcasm. Suddenly he felt as if he'd been baptized in jealousy, as if any moment he would turn green and glow in the night.

"No, Sheriff, she did not. She just came along from Wirt and offered to give me a ride home. I walked out there this evening. A nice brisk walk to clear my head and let me think about my sermon. Thought Inez and George would be there since they'd mentioned coming, and I could beg a ride home with them. Just didn't feel like getting my rig out for such a short ride. But Inez must have had something come up. So I'd started walking home when Tilly found me on the side of the road."

"So what were you doing there?" he asked Tilly again.

"Seeing a friend. A male friend. And it's none of your business who he is," she told him.

"Oh, you didn't tell me you were being courted by someone in Wirt. Who is he, Tilly? Please tell me he is a respectable man who doesn't frequent Lucky's," Julius rambled on.

"It's really none of yours or the sheriff's business who he is, what his name is, or how respectable he is. He's my friend and I'm not obligated to tell you any more," she said.

"Well, you don't have to get so snippy." Julius threw up his hands defensively.

"Then I'll bid you both a good night," Ford said coldly. Damn woman, anyway. Had she danced with this other fellow? Had she let him see her in her cotton dress and no shoes? Had she kissed him yet?

"Good night, Sheriff," Julius's tone was just as icy. Tilly had no right to turn on him like she'd done his friend when Johnny had preached against the evils of liquor. One minute she could be so sweet that Julius had half a notion to ask her to a picnic or for a Sunday afternoon ride in his buggy. The next minute she was bitter as vinegar gone bad, and he wished she'd never come to his church again.

They rode in silence after Ford got his vehicle turned around and headed back toward Wirt. Julius folded his hands across his chest and pouted. Matilda Anderson would never know what she'd wrecked with her smarty pants ways. She could have been married to him in the next six months, living the life of a preacher's wife. His influence could cleanse every tainted skeleton in the Anderson closets. People would forget that she had come from moonshiners and was possibly one herself at one time, and had Indian blood to boot. Well, she'd just lost her last chance. Next Sunday he was going to pay particularly close attention to Miss Olivia Traversty. She'd needed someone to comfort her after the terrible ordeal with Red Anderson and Julius had been there to do the job. She was a bit flighty but in a few months and he'd have her attitude adjusted and a proper pastor's wife made from the rough materials he had to work with.

Tilly wished she could have struck herself mute.

Why did she have to aggravate Ford so much? Probably because he kissed and shunned her like she was a loose lady of the night. She'd lashed back and now she was in big trouble. Bigger than she'd been in years because she needed him to come back to her house next Friday night.

Lucky's had been thrown up in less than a week. A thirty-foot square building of rough wood, no paint or windows and two doors. One at the back led into a small storage room lined with shelves where Lucky kept his supplies. The other in the front was where Ford pushed his way inside. Mismatched chairs were pushed up under tables that looked like they'd been rescued from the hog killing barn. Two tables were surrounded by men playing poker. The little stage in one corner sporting a piano and sometimes women who sang and danced was empty that Saturday night.

A long bar ran along the opposite side from the stage. It was Lucky's domain and no one argued the point. Not with a three-hundred-pound man with a head shaved bald and a black mustache curled up on the ends. Ford leaned against the end of the shiny wood, cleaner than anything in the whole place, and ordered a cup of coffee.

Lucky nodded and poured from a blue granite pot he kept going on the wood stove at the far end of the bar. "Cream or sugar?" he asked.

"Neither, tonight. Just something strong enough to bite," Ford told him.

"Fighting with the little woman are you?" Lucky grinned, showing off a gold eyetooth. It had cost him a fortune and been the best investment he'd ever made. He thought it made him look even more formidable than his size. It let people know just how much he was worth.

"Don't have a little woman and you know it," Ford said.

"Yep, but the only thing make a man look like you do is a woman. I know you got some Indian in you, Sheriff. Them high cheekbones and the nose tell me that. Along with your hair and eyes. But most Indians can poker face a man. Bluff him. They can stand right there in front of a man and you'd never know what was on their mind. But you didn't get that from the Indians. Must be some Irish in there somewhere because you look like you'd be able and willing to fight a grizzly bear with one hand tied behind your back. So what's her name?"

"What makes you think it's a woman? Maybe I'm just mad."

"Only two things make a man that mad. Losing their farm at poker and a woman. I didn't see you pullin' up a chair to the poker table. What's her name?"

"Matilda Anderson. Tilly, they call her."

"Well, good lord, man. There's lots of men folks who been in the spot you're in. Tilly Anderson is the richest woman in the county and the prettiest. Why are you mad at her?"

"I think she's running moonshine and I can't prove it," Ford said honestly.

"Tilly? I don't think so. Why would she do that? She's a churchgoing woman. Farming woman."

"You know her?" Ford drew his eyes down.

"Know of her. Don't actually know her. Heard all about her from the men who work for her cousin's husband, Briar Nelson. Ain't a one of them wouldn't give their heart to her. And not for her money, either."

Ford felt the same envy washing over him like a hard rain that he'd first experienced when he was talking to her earlier that evening. "So you really think she's not running 'shine? Who do you get your supply from? I saw her dart in and out of your back door once a few weeks ago?"

"Oh, yeah. Tilly Anderson in my business. Now that would be a calling card. I could tell everyone that she touched the back door and charge admission to let men look at it." He threw back his head and laughed. "And if I had a supply of moonshine, you think I'd tell you anything about it? You're the sheriff, for God's sake. You could own my place in twenty-four hours. Sell it in thirty-six and I'd be out on the street or rotting in your jail. I heard tell that her grandmother made the stuff and sold it in this part of the county. Also heard that her mother learned the trade, but I'm telling you no one could ever swear on it. I had a bar over in Healdton few years back before I started following the boomtown rage. Heard the rumors and never once heard anything to prove it. I think you're chasing your tail, Sheriff."

"Where would she have the stills if she was making it?" Ford asked.

"Got to have water. Got to have a place to hide it. Don't reckon anyone would be stupid enough to keep it on their own land for fear of getting caught and losing what they've got. Maybe somewhere real close to her farm. I don't know. I still think you're wrong."

"Hey," a well-dressed man threw open the door and scanned the room with a hungry eye. "I'm looking for a game of poker, a woman, and a drink."

"Got poker. Women start to sing at ten thirty but that's all they do. And I got hot coffee, cold tea, and Coca-Cola," Lucky said. "Step right in and meet the sheriff, here. Rayford Sloan, Sheriff of Healdton and surrounding area. What's your name?"

"Pete Wiseman." The man stuck out his hand. "Guess it'll be a dull night. I'll take all the money away from the men and spit dust. Give me a cup of coffee."

"Pretty sure of yourself, aren't you?" Ford eyed his three-piece suit, the gold watch fob, and stiff white collar.

"Got to be. Part of the business. Bluff them."

Just like Tilly, Ford thought. *Bluff them.*

Tomorrow he was going hunting for her stills. He was going to prove himself wrong or right so he could have some peace.

Chapter Eight

Tilly shaded her eyes with the back of her hand. The old folks called what they were experiencing Indian summer. One week of stifling hot heat and winter would come on the coattails of a cold north wind and everyone would beg for a few hot days long before they arrived next summer. She took a long sip of water from the gallon jug she'd brought to the field with her and went back to throwing hay bales on the back of Tucker's old wagon.

Two mules stood with their heads down as if they were even flagged out, waiting for her to click the reins and make them walk a little farther up the pasture. She slipped her hands back into work gloves, grabbed her hay hooks and hoisted another bale up on the back of the wagon. Ten more and she could take them to the barn. A good hard day and she'd have the last of it harvested.

"Hard work for such a little woman," Ford's voice boomed over the top of her head about the time she positioned the bale precariously on the stack.

She looked up at him, sitting astride a big black stallion. "What do you want? And why are you riding that horse? And is he for sale?"

"I want you to look me in the eye and tell me you aren't a bootlegger. I'm riding this horse because he's mine and I don't use the sheriff's car for personal business. No, he's not for sale, but I'm sure he'd love to munch on some of that green grass under that pecan tree. So if that's all right with you, I'll stake him out over there while I help you get this hay inside."

"Why would you do that? I'll pay you six times what he's worth." She eyed the horse. She'd never seen such a beauty. "Can I ride him?"

"I'll help you because you need help. Tucker said you did but there's no one to hire. They're all in the oil fields or gone to war." Ford peered down from the horse. "And I wouldn't sell Akhil for a thousand dollars and you cannot ride him."

"Ache Hill? That his name?" Tilly stepped forward and rubbed the horse's nose. He nuzzled down into her hand. She really did want that horse. She wasn't even trying to get back into Ford's good graces so he'd come to her house later that night, but she wouldn't turn down an opportunity when it dropped in her lap.

"You traitor." Ford stepped gracefully from the saddle and led the horse to the shady spot still sporting a nice cropping of green grass.

"A-k-h-i-l," he said as he staked the horse to a stick he slipped effortlessly into the ground. "It's the Indian word for eagle."

"But he's a fine horse. Why would you name him Eagle?" She picked up another bale and hefted it onto the wagon.

"Got good eyes." Ford fell in beside her lifting two bales to her one. "And it also means whole or complete. Akhil and I are a complete force when we go into a town to clean it up."

"So you don't own a car?" she asked.

"Don't need one."

"How much you going to charge me for a day's work?" She had to huff to keep up with his strong arms. In spite of the late September heat wave, something made her shiver just thinking about those muscles putting tension on his shirt sleeves.

"How about supper and some music when we get finished?"

"Why?"

"Because I was raised up on a farm and I love it. Sheriff business makes me soft. This toughens me up. You're pretty strong for a woman." He stacked the final bale. "I'll drive the wagon. Tell me where to go." He hopped up on the seat and extended his hand to help her.

Electricity crackled between their fingers, even through the gloves. Tilly felt a hard blush beginning all the way down her backbone and extending to her cheeks. She only hoped he thought it was the weather and didn't realize just how he affected her. Ford was well aware of the feelings he had when he touched Tilly and would have liked to keep her hand tightly in his, but they weren't courting. Never would be. Lucky had said she didn't have second dates. If he counted the night of the kiss as a first date he was flat out of luck on the rest.

They unloaded and stacked twenty-six bales in the barn on the back side of her property, grabbed another set of hay hooks and went back for more. Two trips later they stopped for sandwiches she'd brought from the house earlier that morning. She'd packed extra hoping that Tucker would feel sorry for her and come to the rescue. She watched Ford eat with more gusto than a hungry hound after a night of coyote hunting and wished she'd brought twice as much. Hells bells, he was a good man to have around a farm. Kept at the work without complaining. Was strong as a longhorn steer. She wondered what else he was good at, other than making her blush. That idea almost made her drop a bale of hay on her foot.

"So shouldn't you be doing sheriff business today?" She made small talk to shake the vision of his muscles from her mind.

"I get a day off every two weeks. Deputy watches the jail and makes sure Red gets fed and has his checker games. Where do you hide your still?" he asked abruptly, hoping that she'd tell him without thinking. She was tired. It was warm. Her stomach was full of good food.

"Under the hay in the barn. Want to move all the bales and find it?"

Ford shook his head. There was no way a still was up under that barn where they'd put the hay. It had a dirt floor, a few stalls for cattle or horses in the winter, a nice big loft, but nothing underneath. "Can't buy that story, Tilly. Why don't you just tell me that you don't have a still? That you don't run bootleg whiskey. I'll believe you if you tell me. Everything about you says that you are honest."

"Why does it matter?" she asked as she picked up her hooks and went back to work. "Would it change me? Would it change you? Would you stop helping me get the hay in the barn?"

"I want to know," he said.

"You answer my questions first," she told him.

They worked in silence for more than an hour. He worried with the questions she'd asked. No, it wouldn't change her. She'd still be the lovely lady who haunted his dreams. It wouldn't change him. He'd still be the part-Indian no respectable white woman would ever want to be caught out in public with. He wouldn't stop helping her get the hay in the barn because he'd said he'd finish the job for supper and music and he stood by his word. But it did matter, damn it. He was the sheriff and it was his duty to clean up an area. Leave it law-abiding when he left. That meant no bootleggers. A place where folks could bring their families and raise their children without fear of a killing on Main Street every day because some husband and father got liquored up and started fighting.

The hot afternoon sun was relentless but by four

o'clock they had all the hay stacked neatly in her barn, guaranteeing that her cattle wouldn't starve in the harsh winter ahead. She unhooked the mules from the wagon and turned them out to pasture while he stacked the final load. Now she'd have a bath, offer him the use of her bathroom, and cook supper while he cleaned up. She went through what was at hand in the kitchen to cook. Maybe sliced fried ham, cottage fries, open up a jar of corn and one of peas. There was half a peach cobbler still on the cabinet for dessert and a plenty of ice to cool down a pitcher of tea.

Dust boiling up halfway down the lane took her attention when she started toward the house. If it was Tucker finally getting around to offering help, she'd invite him to supper too. Maybe if there was a third party, she wouldn't be so enticed to wrap herself up in Ford's arms and never let him leave.

She shaded her eyes with the back of her hand and watched until the vehicle came to a stop. It wasn't Tucker or Clara, the only two people who ever came uninvited to her home—other than Ford Sloan, and he was trying to weasel his way into finding a still, so he didn't count.

"Tilly, I need to talk to the sheriff." The deputy hopped out of the sheriff's car.

"Over there in that barn." She pointed to the one behind the house. "What's the matter?"

"Got a killing in Ragtown. Couple of men started last night playing poker and drinking. Ended a while ago when one of them accused the other of making eyes at one of Lucky's girls."

"Good grief!" Tilly exclaimed and meant it. That meant Ford would be in the jailhouse all evening. Just exactly where she didn't want him to be. She'd agonized over where to send the buyers for their next supply and finally settled on an old empty building right behind the jail. Ford would never think anyone would have enough nerve to use a stump right under his nose. Besides, she figured he really did like her or else he wouldn't be avoiding her like the plague one day and showing up to help with hay the next. If he didn't like her, why would it be so all-fired important to know for sure whether she was a bootlegger?

Lord, it seemed like she was foiled in every blessed thing she tried. The contraband was already waiting in the old building. The jail was supposed to be dark by ten o'clock, what with only Red inside the joint. Now it would be lit up like the sky on the Fourth of July picnic. If her buyers had any sense at all they'd just drive through town and leave it there for another day. She sure wouldn't blame them if they did.

"I'll have to take a rain check on payment for the day's work." Ford followed his deputy to the car. "And one other thing. I turned Akhil out to pasture with your horses. I'll come get him in a couple of days."

"Don't be in any hurry. He'll probably like my place better than the livery stable anyway. I feed better," she told him.

"Don't you make him fat and don't you dare ride him." Ford pointed a finger at her.

"Go take care of your business. I know how to take care of livestock." She pointed right back at him.

When the dust had settled down the lane she went inside the barn closest to the house and closed the door behind her, not bothering to lock it. She slid bales of hay away from the door and went down the narrow staircase to check her stills. She checked the new sproutings, the first step in making 'shine. Granny declared good 'shine started with sproutings. Said it was the only way to make good moonshine. She said the initial step was to convert the cornstarch into sugar by "sprouting" the corn. Three days before, Tilly had placed her corn in the vats, covered it with warm water, and draped a cloth over the container to prevent contamination and conserve heat. The vats were made with a slow-draining hole at the bottom. She'd added water daily as the liquid slowly seeped away from the bottom. When she tossed aside the cheesecloth, the corn had two-inch sprouts.

"Just right," she mumbled. She dipped the corn into shallow bins with wire on the bottom. It was time for that batch to dry.

She moved over to other bins where the corn had already dried and checked it for dampness even though she could tell by looking that it was ready to grind into meal. Before she began grinding the dried sprouts into a fine cornmeal, she cleaned her two vats and put on another twenty-five pounds of corn to sprout. She could do each step of the job without even thinking about it so her mind went to Ford and where he was at that time. Probably starving half to death from working all afternoon and going without supper. He was a good sheriff, she had to give him that much.

She filled two pots with water from the underground spring pump and put it on the woodstove to boil. When it bubbled she added it to her new batch of cornmeal, starting a new mash. She'd keep that warm to start the fermentation process. Some folks added yeast to hurry the process but she hadn't been taught that way. Without the yeast, fermentation could require more than ten days, but Granny swore that was what made her recipe the best in the world. That and the fact that she always used one cup of brown sugar.

She checked the mash she already had going. The secret was to keep something going in every step of the process, thus assuring enough pure recipe to sell every Friday night. The mash had stopped bubbling and was ready to run. Granny took great care of her sour mash. She never added things that would make the folks who drank it sick. Never a bit of bleach in her recipe to make it bubble and she never used her mash the full eight times it could be used, either. Said if she couldn't give her buyers one hundred proof liquor, she'd quit the business.

Tilly had seen her toss a teaspoon of 'shine on a fire many times. If it didn't flame just right, that mash was finished and poured out. The mental vision of her wizened little grandmother throwing a spoonful of liquor on the fire brought a smile to Tilly's face.

"I'm so tempted to stop all this, Granny. I really do like that man and I'd like to look him right in the eye and tell him I'm not a bootlegger," she muttered as she worked.

As if her grandmother were sitting on the top of the

crock of mash, she heard the voice to her own heart. "Never let temptation decide your course in life."

"I'd forgotten that adage," Tilly said. "So I'm not to let temptation decide what I'm going to do? I'll have to think on that one." She placed the new sour mash into a cooker, which had a lid that she pasted shut so that the seal could be blown off if the internal pressure became too great. At the top of the cooker was a copper pipe that projected to one side and tapered down from a four- to five-inch diameter and on down to the same diameter as the worm that was about an inch to an inch and a half. Granny had made the worms before she died. She'd taken a twenty-foot length of copper tubing, filled it with sand and coiled it around a fence post. The sand, she'd explained to Tilly, kept the tubing from kinking up while it was being twisted around the fence post. Once the worm was formed, the sand was flushed out. That had been Tilly's job and she'd gotten every grain out or Granny would have had her hide tanned and nailed to the smokehouse door.

Tilly smiled brightly. Granny's words exactly. "If you're going to make the recipe, you've got to have good equipment and it's got to be spotless clean."

She checked the worm, which was placed in a barrel full of cold water and sealed to the end of the arm. They had plenty of water with the underground spring Granny's ancestors had found years ago and had built their barn on the top of. First, in case there was ever a catastrophe like one of those tornadoes sweeping up from Texas. During the war it was a hidey-hole for valuables and people if the Yankees ever got into

Indian Territory with their burning ways. Last, it was perfect for the 'shine business. Good cold water was as essential as good mash. And there it was in abundance.

She checked her fire under the cooker. The ethanol vaporized at one hundred and seventy-three degrees, which was the target temperature for the mixture. It was nearing that temperature. The spirit would soon rise to the top of the cooker, enter the arm, and be cooled to the condensation point in the worm. The resulting liquid was collected at the end of the worm into her jars. The fluid was about the color of dark beer and would be returned to the still and cooked again.

Still thinking about Ford and wondering who was being taken to the undertaker and who was in jail, she picked up a small glass vial and began the final test on another batch. She filled it with the liquid and watched the small bubbles rise when she tilted the vial. She positioned it so half the bubbles were above the top level of the liquid and half were below. The proof was approximately one hundred. She'd filter this batch through charcoal and it would be ready for next week's sale. It was dusky dark when she went back outside. She was amazed that so much time had elapsed and so little had been decided. She wanted answers and she was sure she'd find them in the cellar, but she hadn't. What had Katy's memories been trying to tell her when she remembered that old adage about not letting temptation decide on her course of life? She was tempted to stop the bootleg business, but would that make a big difference in her course in life?

Yes, it would. Definitely. Was she ready for that?

She didn't have an answer. She fixed herself a light supper of scrambled eggs and bacon and wondered if she should go into town and waylay her buyers to tell them they were taking their lives in their hands if they tried to pick up their supply. No, she couldn't do that without giving away her identity and that was the number one rule Granny had taught her. By seven thirty she had bathed, donned a pretty dress and one of her famous little wisps of nothing hats and was in the Sweet Tilly headed for the Morning Glory. She needed to talk to Beulah and Bessie one more time before she made up her mind to do something drastic.

She found them both sitting on the porch. Beulah in the white rocker and Bessie in the oversized oak one. She pulled up the third one and began to rock with them without saying a word for the first five minutes.

"What's on your mind, sweetie?" Bessie finally asked.

"You know what we were talking about the other day?" Tilly asked.

"My body might be getting old but my mind is sharp as a tack. I know what we were discussing. Have you changed your mind?"

"Well, I might just until he's gone. Be hard to get my customers back though, so I've got to give it a long hard thinking," Tilly said.

"Darlin', there'll be customers for that or for what a brothel offers any time. They'll be standing in line for those kind of products." Beulah leaned forward and patted her arm. "Me and Bessie got out of it. Katy kept it up until the day she died. Just follow your conscience."

"I remembered something Granny said to me. 'Don't

let temptation decide your course of life.' What if I shut it down and it decides a course of life I'll hate five years down the road?"

"Well, me and Bessie, we been tempted to buy you out, have the stills moved here in the middle of the night and start up a business in the basement of the Morning Glory. Only thing is we don't have that underground spring and I got a feeling folks would start to suspect us if the whole area began to smell like sour mash. Out there in the country the smell gets mixed up with the pig crap and horse manure and all those filthy oil well odors and no one even notices. But to answer your question about what Katy said, Lord have mercy, I've heard her say that a million times. I just think you ought to shut it down for a spell and see how things go. You can go back to it when the time is right. That sheriff is going to take you down, girl, if you don't. I know it in my old bones and I'm scared for you."

"Bessie?" Tilly asked. "I got enough going now to make it through three weeks of deliveries. You think I should shut it down after that?"

"No, before that. You got the buyers picking up tonight?"

Tilly nodded.

"Where?"

"Old grocery store building. That one that hasn't been in business since I was a little girl."

"Good God, Matilda Jane. That's within spitting distance of the jail." Bessie stopped rocking and shivered so hard her bones rattled. "What are you trying to do? Get caught?"

"No, I'd planned on enticing the sheriff to come out to my place for the evening. At least the back door isn't visible from the front of the jail."

"And you couldn't entice him?" Beulah's eyes widened.

"There was a killing in Ragtown. He had to go be a lawman," Tilly said.

"Okay, nothing to be done about it now. They'll be picking up their stash about ten, right?" Beulah's voice was high and squeaky.

Tilly nodded again.

"Well, you get on down to the jailhouse. I've got fresh cookies made in there and you're going to take them to Red. If the sheriff can't be enticed by that red dress you're wearing, he's half dead. And the way that man is built, honey, he's all the way alive. Take the cookies and make up some story about how you didn't want to bring them. That'll throw him off the track. And you keep him busy until after ten. I'm going to slip in the back door and tear up your notes. The new ones are going to say you're out of the business for a few weeks. Sheriff is putting too much heat on and that this batch is free. So you aren't even to go near that place to get your money." Bessie braced her hands on the rocker arms and grunted when she stood up.

"But . . ." Tilly stammered.

"You don't need the money and you know it. Go home and shut it down tomorrow. No more sprouts. No more mash. Not another batch until he's gone for good. Katy would expect us to take care of you. Lord, honey, times is changing. Law is getting worse and worse. Couldn't buy them honest lawmen if you wanted to. We've all made a fortune with those stills. It's time to move along to something else."

"Like a boardinghouse?" Tilly asked.

"Girl, this is good honest living that Ford Sloan won't take away from us," Beulah said. "Now you follow the instructions. Lawsy me, I can't believe you've got a whole run in that building. That's even worse than the church outhouse."

Tilly felt like she should be angry. Or disappointed. Or both. Her heart should be clenched up in a knot just thinking about giving up what had been in her family for generations. She should be in tears. But all she felt was relief. She'd have hours and hours more in the day to take care of the farm, to keep house better even if she did despise housework, to spend time with Libby and Clara.

"Okay, here's the cookies." Bessie held out a small tin bucket.

"Thanks. I mean it. For the first time in my life, I didn't know what to do." Tilly helped herself to a cookie and munched on it as she walked down the street toward the jail. She'd purposely left the Sweet Tilly in front of the boardinghouse so that her story about the cookies would hold up in Ford's court.

She peeked in the window of the jail. Ford was sitting at his desk, a mountain of paper in front of him. He still wore the work clothes he'd had on all day and there were smudges of dirt around his ears. The only difference was he'd thrown on his vest with the big star pinned to the left side, making him a sheriff instead of a farmer.

She pushed open the door and said, "Hello."

He jumped as if he'd been shot with a double barrel from a short distance. "What are you doing in town?"

"I came to see the ladies at the Morning Glory since you couldn't stay for supper and dancing," she smiled. "Bessie made me bring these cookies for Red. She feels sorry for him."

"She made you?" He raised an eyebrow and wished he'd had time to clean up. She looked cool in spite of the hot Indian summer night breeze. He wished he could cross the room, take her in his arms, inhale deeply of the perfume he knew she wore and kiss her until they were both breathless.

"Yes, she made me, if you must know. I'd had enough of you all day long. I was even glad to see you go so I didn't have to cook supper for you," she lied, and childishly crossed her fingers behind the bucket.

"Well, Red is back there complaining because he has to put up with a new inmate. Joe Tanner from down in Louisiana. Come up here to work the oil wells and ended up killing a man. Says it was self-defense. Man drew a knife on him," Ford said.

"So you'll see to it he gets these?" She set the bucket on the desk.

"No, I won't. I might eat every one of them myself. I'm starving half to death," Ford said.

"Why haven't you eaten? Man is behind bars. He ain't going nowhere."

"I'm plannin' on it. Was just about to go down to the hotel and see if they've got anything left in the kitchen. Want to join me?" he asked. By golly, she had something other than cookies and a prisoner on her mind. His gut feeling said so, and he trusted that more than anything else. She might be turning the tables and following him around to make sure he was tied down before she went off to do a little bootlegging.

"Sure," she said.

"Really?" he was amazed. Every single thing kept saying she wasn't a moonshiner and yet there was that feeling in his heart that said she was.

"I said I would, didn't I? Tell you what. You go wash the dirt off your face and I'll give these to Red. I'll just set them on the floor so he can reach out and get them. I wouldn't ask for the keys. If he escaped, you'd try to take my car away from me."

"I don't think I could take your car unless I found bootleg whiskey in it." Ford laughed at her misunderstanding of the law. "But you can take the cookies back and I'll be back down in five minutes."

"Deal but not a date."

"Oh, and here I thought you were chasing me for my good looks and dancing abilities."

"Lawman, I'm not chasing you. You're following me and running into me so often I'm beginning to sport bruises, but I'm not chasing you. You are certainly not my type."

"And you aren't mine, either," he retorted as he picked up the keys to the cells and carried them with him. "Not that I don't trust you, but I wouldn't want you to be tempted to break Red out of jail."

"Thank you. I sure wouldn't want to be tempted to turn loose a robber and a killer onto the fine society of Healdton, Oklahoma. I'll be waiting and please hurry. I'm starving too."

He was back in just over five minutes. They strolled down Main Street to the hotel where there was indeed some pot roast and fresh bread still available, and wonder of wonders, two slices of coconut cream pie. They ate fast and furious, Tilly not owning up to the fact she'd already had a makeshift supper of eggs and bacon.

"So, how about a game of checkers?" Ford nodded toward a table in the far corner that had just been vacated by a couple of oil men. She wasn't going to snow him into letting her go take care of her illegal business. Placate him with a pretty face, a sexy hat, nice dress, soft, Southern voice, and leave him to think about her while she delivered moonshine. No, sir, he'd keep her busy until it was too late for her to do anything but go home or stay at the Morning Glory the rest of the night. Which he fully well intended to suggest.

"I'm damn good at checkers. Tucker couldn't beat me from the time I was three years old. Want to put a dollar on the game?" she asked. She'd keep him in the hotel until past ten o'clock and she fully well intended to stay in the spare room at the Morning Glory, just to make him wonder if he was wrong about her night-time business.

The clock in the lobby chimed ten times when she yawned. "Bessie and Beulah asked me to stay the night and have breakfast with them in the morning," she explained.

"I'll walk you," he said gallantly.

"That would be very nice." She would keep him on the porch a few minutes, giving her buyers a few extra minutes to get out of town.

When they reached the inn, she sat down in a rocking chair and patted the one next to her. "Looks like everyone is already in bed. Might as well enjoy the warm night a few minutes. In another week, a blue norther will bluster in and we'll be wishing for a time when we could sit on the porch."

"People are going to talk, Tilly." Ford leaned against a porch post.

"That bother you?"

"No, but it's your reputation at stake."

"If I remember right, it was you who put me in jail and ruined my good name to begin with. Calling me a bootlegger and having Inez all stirred up. You know I think she's got a crush on you."

"Great thunder. She's married."

"Don't matter. She's all flitty and flirty when you're around. People might start talking about that if you aren't careful."

"On that note, I'm going home. Thanks for having supper with me and thanks for the checker game. I'll collect my dollar another time."

"I let you win." She stood up.

"You did not. You just met your match."

"Believe it if you want to, honey. And I'll bring your dollar to church on Sunday."

She took a step to go inside. He took one toward the porch and they were chest to chest without meaning to be. She looked up. He leaned down and their lips met in the middle as if they had a mind of their own. Tingles danced all over her body. She wanted to stop and analyze the feelings but didn't want the kiss to end. Was this the temptation Granny had warned her about? Not the temptation of making 'shine but of some man turning her insides into a quivering mass of mush?

Ford drew away first. "Good night, Tilly. I'll collect that dollar on Sunday."

"That all you got to say?"

"What do you want me to say? A kiss doesn't mean I have to make an honest woman out of you. I didn't keep you out all night. I didn't make any promises with it. A nice kiss, but just a kiss."

"You are a rogue," she whispered.

"Been called worse," he said as he left her standing in the dark.

The clock chimed once from in the house. It was ten thirty.

Red was enjoying oatmeal cookies and wondering why in the devil Bessie had sent them, yet not begrudging his good luck one bit when he heard someone behind the jail. Walking fast. Muttering. Red grabbed two cookies and stood on the cot to look outside. It was Bessie from down at the Morning Glory

Inn. Good grief, what on earth was that old woman doing out at that time of night?

He watched her look both ways and disappear into the old grocery store building back behind the jail. A soft light filtered through the dirty windows but only for a few minutes. Bessie reappeared and retraced her footprints. He noticed this time that she carried a lantern with her.

Curiosity got the best of him. He forgot all about the cookies and watched as an automobile eased down the street behind the jail. Things might be still going strong out on the edge of town at the bars but it wasn't usual to hear traffic at ten o'clock at night so close to the jail. Especially when an elderly lady had just spent some time in that same building. The car pulled into the alleyway. Two men went in and came back out carrying something under wraps that appeared to be heavy.

"Well, I'll be damned." Red chuckled.

"What's so funny?" Joe demanded, the liquor wearing off and the headache setting in. "Don't you laugh at me. You robbed a bank. You got to stay in here for a year. I'll be out soon as they figure out I was only actin' in self-defense."

"Nothing to do with you. Want a cookie? Help yourself." Red motioned toward the bucket.

"It'd just come back up," Joe said and began to snore almost immediately.

Red watched two wagons make stops at the building, collect their merchandise, another car and a truck. Each time he chuckled harder. So it was true. And

Bessie and Beulah knew it. They were covering for her and that's why he got cookies. So she could entice the sheriff away from the jail.

The last vehicle had just left when he heard the sheriff returning from a late supper. Red picked up two more cookies from the bucket and stretched out on the cot.

"Everything all right back here?" Ford asked.

"I think old Joe is going to be sick," Red said.

"Joe, you asleep?"

Snores answered him.

"Have a cookie, Sheriff. Bessie does make a good oatmeal cookie. Wonder why she sent them to me, though? Never knew the woman to be that nice to me," Red said.

"You sure are talkative tonight." Ford reached for a cookie.

"You have a good time with Tilly?"

"Had supper. Played checkers. Walked her home to the Morning Glory. I'm about to decide she's not into bootlegging and that Inez is just telling tales."

"Told you to cut that woman's tongue out. Night, Sheriff."

"Wait a minute. Why were you so full of words tonight?"

"Guess it was the cookies. Brought out the words."

"I'll have to have Bessie make some more. They are pretty good," Ford said as he ate one and carried another one toward his desk.

"Good as that kiss you had with Tilly?"

"How'd you know that?"

"Well, if you don't want someone to know you kissed Tilly, you'd better suck on a lemon."

"Why would I suck on a lemon?"

"To wipe that grin off your face. Cookies is wearing off. I'm going to sleep." Red shut his eyes.

Chapter Nine

Inez Simpson removed the rag rollers from her hair and fluffed out the curls with a silver-handled brush. She stared long and hard at the woman in the mirror above her chest of drawers. She'd never be the beauty that Tilly Anderson was, or even Clara, but she liked what she saw. There was fire in her eyes, determination in her jaw, and confidence in her chin. Things she should have had all those years ago when her mother said she would marry George whether she loved him or not. She gently laid the brush in her suitcase with the rest of the dresser set her mother had given her for a wedding gift. It would always remind her that a pretty bit of metal couldn't bring happiness, and to never listen to another person. She applied bright red lipstick, the color George hated, and opened a brand-new pot of rouge, another thing he despised. But today wasn't about her husband or his likes and dislikes.

Today Inez was thirty-two and after she made one stop at the jailhouse, she'd never see George again.

She chose her best blue Sunday dress. Julius would be aghast when he discovered what she'd done. So would the rest of the proper population in Healdton, but if they hadn't wanted their women folks eyeing the handsome, young virile oil men they shouldn't have sold the leases to their land. It wasn't all her fault, she rationalized. She'd married at sixteen. George was twenty-five. Her mother had pushed for the match since George had just inherited the drugstore from his father. Security, her mother called it. Love didn't matter. She could come to respect George and he'd do right by her. Half a lifetime later Inez was giving up her good-girl security for a life of excitement and passion, one way or the other.

She opened the door to a blustery, rainy fall day. But even the cold wind and chill of the rain couldn't dampen her spirits. She threw a rain cape around her shoulders, stuck her hands out the slits and picked up an umbrella. Thirty minutes. One stop. Then she'd be ready for Sonny to pick her up. The note was written to George and lying on his dresser. Gossip would run rampant, whatever the day brought. She liked the idea of leaving town mysteriously, living in Ardmore or Oklahoma City under an assumed name while she waited on Ford to sell that big black horse of his, invest in a car and take her away to somewhere exotic like Savannah, Georgia. She even toyed with approaching Julius. He had to be enamored with her, the way he always sought out her advice on every little thing. But that was just a passing fancy. Preachers didn't run away with married women. Sonny might be the last of her choices, but he was the most passionate. Coming into the drugstore for a lemonade every evening. Talking about his work, his misfortunes, his need to have a good woman in his life. He'd been the one to make the offer that set her to thinking there was something better than Healdton and making lemonade while George worked the pharmacy.

Ford stood up with a sigh when the jailhouse door blew open, not expecting anyone would be coming in, but blaming the wind for shaking loose the latch for the third time that morning. He practically collided with Inez when she backed into the office, umbrella and slicker both dripping.

"Good morning," he said.

"Ford, I've come to tell you what happens when you don't listen to me. Last weekend, while you were out having your sweet little supper with Matilda Anderson there was a moonshine deal going down right in your back door. Literally. In the old grocery store building. I was sitting in my bedroom window. Couldn't sleep so I was watching the street from the apartment we have above the store. And there went Bessie from down at the Morning Glory Inn. I always said she had too much money for it to be legal. Well, the old woman went with a lantern into the building, stayed a few minutes and went back to the inn. In a matter of minutes, five different people came by and carried something out of that building. I counted them. Five. One truck. Two cars. And two wagons. Right under your nose and you couldn't catch them."

"You're telling me Bessie is running 'shine?" he asked incredulously.

"Probably making it in the basement. Changing her pickup place every week and just forgot something. Bet she left some kind of note," Inez said excitedly. "Want me to go with you to check it out? And I'd be willing to bet that Tilly is in on the deal too."

"You can't be serious." Ford bit the inside of his lip to keep from laughing.

"Yes, I am. She and Beulah both were rumored to have been tied up with Katy Anderson's moonshine business. No one could ever prove it but they're two slick old girls. You'd do well to check out that boarding-house. I bet Clara was in on the whole operation too."

"I'll have a talk with Bessie. Probably find out she lost a cat and was out looking for it," he said.

"Sure she did, and that cat's name is bootleg whiskey," Inez snapped.

"I thank you for the information." Ford tried to be polite.

"Ford, I've got something else to say. I'm leaving George." She looked at the watch pin attached to the lapel of her dress. "In fifteen minutes my ride will be here. I'm sick of this town and I'm going. Can you give me one good reason why I should stay?" She pushed back her hair, tucked it behind her ear, and brazenly looked him right in the eye.

He felt high color filling his cheeks. Was the woman

making a play for him? The sheriff? Right there in broad daylight with two prisoners within hearing distance. "I would think that's a question you would need to ask George," he finally said.

"George is already out of the picture. It's a question I'm asking you. Give me a good reason and Sonny can go right on down the road to Burkburnett, Texas all by himself."

"I suppose I can't," Ford said.

"Good-bye, Sheriff Sloan. I know you will miss my invaluable help with your mission to clean up the area of illegal moonshiners, but it's a decision you have made. Give me a reason to stay. Tell me what I want to hear and together we'll make a fantastic team," she said.

"What do you want to hear?" He wanted to bite his tongue off when he heard the words coming out of his mouth.

"If you have to ask you don't feel the same things I do." She popped open the umbrella and left the door wide open when she left.

Ford sat there in stunned silence, the clean smell of a fall rain wafting in from outside. Surely he'd just dreamed all that. She couldn't have been serious about Bessie. Tilly, he could see running bootleg. She was young, determined, and headstrong. Bessie was an old woman who made cookies for prisoners and knitted sweaters while she rocked on the front porch.

He pinched his leg. It hurt. He hadn't dreamed any of it, not even the almost-declaration of love from Inez Simpson. The woman was touched in the head just like Red had said in his single-syllable sentences.

"Told you to cut her tongue out," Red said from the jail cell. "She's crazy and Sonny ain't no better."

"Know the man?"

"Very well. He's from down in north Texas. Had a wife but she died. Got six or eight kids a sister's been keeping for him. Inez might be beggin' George to take her back in the sight of a week."

"You're right talkative again today. Still munching on cookies?" Ford asked.

"No, ate them all that night."

Ford laughed aloud.

Tilly stood in the middle of the basement, staring at several lifetimes of bootlegger's equipment. Starting with the corn, she drained the water from the vats and planned to feed all twenty-five pounds to the hogs. She wasn't sure what to do with the mash, which was barely into the fermentation stage. The hogs could probably eat that too. What was ready to be distilled she could simply pour out, but where? Never once since the cellar had been set up to make whiskey had they ever had the need to throw anything away. Granny lived by the "waste not, want not" rule. It would have been right next-door to pure sin to let a mash go too long, to let the temperature get too high in the distilling process, or anything that would prevent a batch from reaching maturity.

She went upstairs and out of the barn, found a couple of five-gallon galvanized buckets and went back to fill them for the hogs. Several trips later, she was exhausted and not totally convinced she was doing the right thing since she'd slept on it. Perhaps Granny's advice about not letting temptation decide the course of your life was telling her to keep right on doing what she was and not be tempted to stop. No, that couldn't be right. Bessie and Beulah were wise old owls and they'd given her solid advice.

When the last of the stills was clean, she sat down at the grinding table and crossed her arms over the rough wood, laid her head down and wept. An era had just ended and for what? A few kisses from a sheriff? What on earth had she just done? She wiped away her tears, took a look around and wondered if she'd ever feel alive again like she did when she took chances with bootleg whiskey. The thrill. The chase. Outsmarting several lawmen including one Sheriff Rayford Sloan. Was there anything out there to put an extra beat in her heart?

Her heart was heavier than the bales of hay she shoved over the door, hiding it from everyone. Not even Clara or Tucker had ever been down in that basement. They knew it was there but neither of them ever showed an interest in the process and admission wasn't granted to anyone who wasn't serious about learning the business. She was bone tired when she reached the house. She soaked in a warm bath until the water turned cold and had barely gotten dressed in the blue housedress Ford had found her wearing when she saw the car coming up the driveway. She stepped out on the porch, inhaled the clean air from a good old morning downpour, and wondered if Ford was playing the shadow game again. Was he coming around to demand full payment for helping her with the hay? Or maybe to take Akhil back to town? The first she'd abide. It wouldn't take much to fry a slab of ham and make a big man-sized omelet, put some biscuits in the oven, and make a little sausage gravy. But she fully well intended to fight him on the horse business. That big boy needed a pasture to kick up his heels, not a stall where he'd grow fat and lazy.

"Hi." Clara opened the door of her brand-new car and hopped out. "Hadn't seen you all week and thought I'd better come by. Besides, I've got gossip. You got coffee or cake?"

"Just made coffee. No cake. Brought home some of Bessie's cookies but they're a little stale. Come on in. I could use some good gossip or even a little company. I just shut down my illegal business."

Clara missed the bottom step and stumbled up the rest before she regained balance. "You did what? Why? Did Ford find out too much?"

Tilly grabbed her cousin's arm and looped her own through it. "No, nothing like that. I've had that man chasing his tail so much, he don't know if he's coming or going. I talked to Bessie and Beulah last weekend and they were adamant about it. Two old heads like that know more than I ever will. But mainly it was because every time I turned around I was almost caught. *Almost,* I said." She led Clara into the kitchen and pulled out a chair. She found two cups and saucers and brought the coffeepot to the table, along with a plate of cookies.

"Well, it'll sure make me breathe easier. I've been

terrified since that episode with Red. It all going down right there behind Ford the whole time. And the business in the church outhouse. Lord, Tilly, what were you thinking?"

"It sounded like the perfect place until everything went to hell in a handbasket," Tilly said. "Anyway, it took me all day but the basement doesn't have a corn kernel or a bit of mash in it."

"You know you could get in big trouble just having those stills, don't you?" Clara reminded her.

"Yes, I do. But everyone in the state knows Granny ran bootleg so I could always say the stills belonged to her and I didn't have the muscle or brawn to move them out," she said.

"You might fool Ford since he's a sucker for you," Clara said.

"What are you talking about?"

"Well, he is. Can't take his eyes off you when you're around. Briar says he's been bit by the marriage bug." Clara picked up a second cookie.

"Briar is crazy as an old gray outhouse rat." Tilly's cheeks sported two red circles the size of silver dollars.

"You be careful talking about my husband like that." Clara shook her finger at Tilly. "And now for the gossip. Inez ran off with an oil man. One who's got six or eight kids and who's taking her to Burkburnett, Texas. Name of Sonny. He works for Magnolia."

Tilly spewed coffee and cookies halfway across the table. "Inez Simpson?" she stammered the name out in four drawn-out syllables.

"Yep, went to the jail and asked Ford if he could

think of any reason for her to stay before she and Sonny took off. They say George isn't talking about it. Says he just hopes she's happy."

"Well, it never was a match made in heaven. George's daddy wasn't leaving his business to a man without a wife to keep him stable. Inez's mother pushed her into the marriage because she was afraid the girl would disgrace the family with her flirty ways and gossiping tongue. I remember when she married George. I felt sorry for both of them. Granny and I went to the wedding. Neither of them looked all dewy-eyed and happy. Nothing like the day Briar and you left town. Love oozed out of both of you."

Clara smiled. "Did you hear what I said? She went to give Ford first chance at running away with her."

"She did what? Did he tell you that?" The red spots were back on Tilly's cheeks.

"No, but Red told Bessie when she brought him another batch of cookies. I saw her today when I went to town. She says that Red told her the whole thing and she intends to take him cookies at least once a week to find out what he knows."

"And Inez just strolled in there and offered to run off with Ford?" Tilly couldn't believe her ears.

"That's what Red said. Ford was gone out to check on the old grocery store building when Bessie came in so he could tell it all."

"The old grocery store building? Why would he do that?"

"Seems Inez told him that Bessie was the one running bootleg in town and she saw her from her bedroom window up above the store going in there late last weekend. The night you and Ford put up hay and had supper together at the hotel. Anyway, Inez blew the whistle on Bessie and he went to investigate. Bessie thinks it's a hoot. Hopes he comes to the Morning Glory and demands to search it. That way he'll know for sure that Inez was just gossiping. She didn't tell me that you were shutting down, though."

"She and Beulah knew. That's why Bessie went to the old grocery store building. To put a note on the supplies telling the buyers that I wasn't going to make any more until the heat died down."

"Want to drive into town and see if he did go search the inn?" Clara's eyes twinkled.

"Where's Libby and Briar?"

"Oh, they're fine. Briar drove her over to Ardmore for ice cream at the fancy hotel lobby so I could come spread gossip."

"Good lord, that man is in love with you, Clara! Drive a child more than twenty miles just to buy ice cream."

"Oh, it wasn't just for that. He had business about some leases. The oil men keep rooms there, you know, so they can wheel and deal. It's a twofold venture, but Libby doesn't know it and I pretended ignorance. That way he gets what he wants. Libby gets her father for the evening. And I get to visit."

"How'd you get so smart? Seems like it wasn't even a year ago you were going to town every day and sitting on a bench outside the drugstore waiting on a fool man to come back and elope with you," Tilly reminded her.

"No, darlin', I was waiting on the fool man to come back every day for ten years so I could take my little gun out of my purse and shoot the sorry sucker dead," Clara told her. "Now, are you going to town with me or not?"

"Wouldn't miss it for a . . ." she stopped midsentence. She'd almost said "for a kiss from the handsome sheriff," but she wasn't ready to share that with Clara. Not just yet anyway, and besides, she wasn't over the jolt of jealousy that rose up to gag her when she thought of Inez Simpson trying to sneak Rayford Sloan away from her.

"For what?" Clara grinned.

"Nothing. I'll go get dressed. Be back in five minutes and I'll drive."

"I bet it was nothing." Clara poured another cup of coffee. Five minutes for Tilly lasted at least fifteen and maybe twenty if she thought Ford might be at the Morning Glory Inn. She wasn't fooling Clara one bit when she feigned disinterest in Ford. There had never been a man who'd kept Tilly's interest for more than two hours, but there'd never been a man who'd disagreed with her either. The men around Healdton would lay facedown in a mud puddle and let her walk on their backs so she wouldn't get her pretty little shoes dirty.

Bessie watched the sunset from the rocking chair on the porch, like she did most evenings except when it was bitter cold. Seemed that her old bones didn't cotton to the winter anymore and it didn't take much to put a chill in her. Doctors and folks could think and say what they wanted but an old body like hers could catch pneumonia from the cold weather, and even if it wasn't so, she wasn't taking chances at her age.

She wasn't surprised to see the Sweet Tilly come to a stop in front of the inn about dusk. Tilly would have been working all day in the basement. Mercy, but she and Katy and Beulah had enjoyed some fine times down there in that cellar. They'd solved the world's problems as well as the local ones. Cussed and discussed their husbands. Cried on each other's shoulders over their children. Probably, if the truth be told, it was their camaraderie while they worked that kept their marriages from going down the outhouse hole. It wouldn't have been easy for Tilly to take care of that job. Physically or mentally.

Bessie had deliberately told Clara the gossip earlier so she'd go by and keep Tilly company that evening. Old fools meddling. That's what Beulah said, but she didn't fool Bessie one bit. If she hadn't meddled, Beulah would have. *Well, well, well,* Bessie thought. *I'll just barely get them settled in when the sheriff will arrive. Things sure are easy to get done when you're old and everyone thinks you're senile.*

"Evening." Clara plopped down into a rocking chair.

"What brings you two to town?" Bessie asked innocently.

"We come to see if Ford is going to search the inn," Clara told her.

"I expect he'll have to since Inez couldn't keep her big mouth shut. One last blast of hot air before she left. What could that woman be thinkin' about, trying to get the sheriff to say he'd fallen in love with her? Good grief! Anybody got a lick of sense knows that man ain't got eyes for Inez Simpson," Bessie said.

"Well, speak of the devil and he shall appear," Tilly whispered as she saw Ford coming up the walk. The long-legged gait, the cut of his jaw, the way he combed his hair worn straight back, the tight fit of the vest, and the shine of the star pinned on it combined to heat up every nerve in her body. She didn't know if she was ready to kiss him or fight him.

"Mornin' ladies." Ford nodded. "Bessie, I've had a complaint that you might be running a little bootleg right out of this establishment. I think the woman who's been spreading such things has beans for brains, but I have to ask. All you have to do is tell me it isn't true. I'll believe you because I consider you a lady of virtue and one who wouldn't lie to me."

"Rayford Sloan, you are a fool of a man and a sorry sheriff. I've run bootleg in the past and if I wanted to run it now, darlin', you'd be hustlin' to find my stills or my stumps. Don't never believe a woman unless she's kissin' you and sayin' she loves you. All else you take care of proper. Now I haven't made or sold a mason jar of 'shine since you were nothing but a schoolboy, but you're going to search this place from top to bottom. When the gossip vine goes to sproutin' leaves and growin' come daylight, you'll be able to say you done took care of it right and there's not even the remnants of a worm or an old still anywhere on this place. Tilly is going to go with you. Start at the top. There's a lantern on the bottom step up to the attic. It's full of fuel and it'll throw a good light. I cleaned the chimney right good when I heard what garbage Inez was puttin' out this morning."

"Yes, ma'am," Ford said seriously. "But Clara might do a better job of showing me around since she's the one who owned the place."

"Clara is going to sit right here with me and tell me about that handsome husband of hers and that pretty little daughter she got in the bargain. Tilly ain't got a thing to tell me so she can go with you. Besides, she knows every crook and cranny of this old house as good as Clara. She spent lots of time here in her growing up years. Every week her momma or her granny would bring her in to play for the day. So get along with you. You too, Tilly. Do I need to send Beulah with you so's you'll have a chaperone and you won't be havin' to make an honest woman out of her come daylight? That old lock up to the attic sticks real bad. Hate for you to shut the door and spend the night up there together."

"Bessie!" Tilly was sincerely shocked.

"Get on with you. I ain't got time for no sass." Bessie pointed toward the door. She'd done her part now. They could fight or sneak a kiss. She hoped it was the latter.

Somehow Tilly felt like she'd been hoodwinked. Clara showing up and wanting to go to the Morning Glory Inn. Too much had happened to be mere coincidence, yet, how could any of them have known the time Ford would arrive? None of it made a bit of sense.

"This way, lawman. Up one flight and to the end of the hall where there's a narrow passage up to the attic. We'll start there and you'll have your proof that there's not a distillery in the Morning Glory Inn." Tilly led the way.

"I know there's not. This is just to make Bessie look good." The deep tone of his voice melted her insides into a trembling mass.

Tilly lit the lantern and held it high. All they found were trunks of old books and clothing. Toys she and Clara had played with all those years ago. A rocking chair and a baby cradle. A dress form Clara's mother must have used to make clothing for herself. No mash vats. Not even a single grinder for corn.

They took a quick look in each bedroom after knocking. Nellie and Cornelia thought it was a big laugh. Inez, they declared, had done George a favor when she ran away because she only had half a brain if she thought there was a still in the Morning Glory or that Bessie would condone such a thing. Lord, she was so straightlaced, she didn't even permit the Sears Catalog to be left in the parlor because it had pictures of ladies' unmentionables in it. That would be improper if a gentleman came calling on one of the school teachers or Olivia.

"So I hear Inez proposed to you today," Tilly said when they walked through the dining room and out into the kitchen. "Now here you would find the proper things to make whiskey. Pans. A stove. Running water. But smell deeply. Really sniff hard. Not a single sour mash aroma in the whole room. A place this size would reek of it, Sheriff."

"Who told you Inez proposed?" His neck prickled with the heat. "And I know what sour mash smells like, Tilly. I'm not a greenhorn. Oklahoma entered the union as a dry state ten years ago. I had my first job in a little town north of here. I cleaned up more stills than you can imagine those two years."

"It's all over town that you broke her little heart so she took off with Sonny. Now why'd you do that to a good man like Sonny? And when you cleaned up those stills did you wash them down good? Make sure all the whiskey was out of the worm so it wouldn't rot the copper?"

"I didn't think about doing anything mean to Sonny." Ford made a pretense of looking under the kitchen sink for a hidden still. "I was just so worried about those little children with no momma. I thought they needed Inez worse than me. And honey, you know damn good and well what I'm talking about when I say I cleaned up a still. When I got finished the worms were tangled and kinked and the stills weren't good for anything."

"You knight in shining armor. I'm sure those little kids are all going to write you a long letter of praise and glory. They may name a new book in the Bible after you. Call it the glorious gospel of Ford Sloan."

"Just couldn't run away with another man's wife." Ford followed her down to the basement. "Seemed harsh to send her on her way with Sonny but truth is

I'm in love with another woman. She's stole my heart away with her good cooking and honesty."

Tilly stopped dead in her tracks and turned so fast she had to brace herself to keep from stumbling over an ancient kitchen chair with only three legs. Ford reached out and grabbed her by the shoulders, looking down into those blue eyes that captivated him. He was an inch away from kissing her when she leaned away from him, looked up into his dark, smoldering eyes and asked, "Who is this woman?"

"Bessie," he said seriously.

"And what gives you hope of her even noticing you?" A giggle erupted from her chest and wouldn't stop.

"Because she was throwing rocks at me out there. Telling me I was a fool sheriff if I didn't search the house. That's what girls do when they like boys. They throw rocks at them and say mean things. I think she likes me."

"Crazy as it might seem, I think she does too," Tilly turned around and held the lantern high. She didn't think she could bear kissing him again and going home to nothing.

Chapter Ten

Tilly didn't hear a word the preacher said. In her peripheral vision she saw the flutter of a lace-trimmed hanky as Beulah wiped away tears. Libby sobbed. Briar sat stoically. Ford sat in front of her, along with the other pallbearers, his back ramrod straight. His thick black hair made a distinct contrast to the starched white shirt collar.

She'd retreated back to that place of numbness inside her heart she reserved for times when she couldn't face the pain. The last time she'd visited that dim room at the core of her being had been when her Granny died. Clara and Tucker had expected her to collapse in a bundle of raw screaming nerves. She hadn't. True to her heritage, she'd held her head high and made it through the wake, the funeral and the days afterward. No one knew about the days and nights she spent sitting in Katy's bedroom, rocking in the creaky old chair, tears streaming down her cheeks while she mourned in private.

Finally, Julius stopped talking. The pallbearers hefted the wooden casket onto their broad shoulders and carried it outside to the hearse. A fine carriage pulled by six white horses. Beulah had insisted on everything being done proper. After the six men finished their job, Beulah, Tilly, Clara, and Tucker took their places inside the hearse. There would be a journey through town, past the Morning Glory Inn, past the place at the edge of town where Bessie had been born, the house she'd lived in when she was married and bore her two sons, and then on to the cemetery. One last long trip for her spirit to remember all the good times. Tilly clutched at the handkerchief in her hands, thinking that they should drive Bessie's remains past her farm so she could say good-bye to the stills that had been a part of her life also.

"She's probably laughing with Granny," Clara whispered.

"Telling her that I shut down the stills," Tilly said hoarsely.

"I'm mad at her," Beulah declared. "She was supposed to wait for me. We were going to surprise Katy by showing up together."

Tilly patted her hand. "They've got to get things ready for you."

"Well, they'd better hurry up because I'm tired," Beulah said.

Folks formed two long lines from the hearse to the open grave. The pallbearers hoisted the casket up on their shoulders and the four who were her special friends walked solemnly behind it. Bessie's last journey from Healdton to heaven. Julius said something else and there was a song and a prayer, but Tilly retreated back inside her soul where memories were stored. The sound of red dirt clods hitting the wooden box brought her back to reality. It was over. Another of the three old girls had left this life and went on to the next.

Tucker led Beulah back to Briar's car where Libby waited in the back seat and Briar leaned on the fender, watching his wife, making sure she wasn't going to collapse. Clara slipped her arm around Tilly and leaned her head on her cousin's shoulder. "Come home with us. Flora is getting supper ready."

"In a little while, maybe. I'll have to stay until it's all done. Bessie would want that, you know. I can't leave her just yet," Tilly said.

"Before dark. Promise you won't stay after dark the way you did before," Clara whispered.

"I promise. Just an hour. I'll be along soon."

Clara left her, just like she'd done when they'd buried Granny. Only that time she'd had to come back at dark to beg Tilly to leave the grave.

Tucker stood beside her for a while. "Tilly, let her go. It was her time. At least she went in her sleep and didn't suffer."

"I'm not ready yet," Tilly said. "Go on home to Clara's. Take Beulah for the afternoon and I'll be along soon."

"There's nothing you can do here." Tucker tried to steer her away from the grave.

She shrugged him away. "I'm staying. I have to do this my way, Tucker. She was my friend. Let me alone for a little while. Just a bit to tell her one last good-bye."

Tucker nodded and went back to Briar's car where he leaned in and talked to the people inside. She couldn't hear the words but Beulah nodded a couple of times and wiped her eyes. Tucker slammed the driver's door and the vehicle moved away from the cemetery. Tilly watched every shovelful of red dirt that filled in the hole and nodded to the grave digger when he left the scene.

She sat down at the head of the grave and patted the loose dirt. Bessie wasn't supposed to be dead. She was supposed to sit on the porch of the Morning Glory and someday Tilly would bring her children to see her. She'd made that promise years ago when Bessie's sons both died of the cholera the same year. Back when Tilly was only sixteen. Ralph was thirty that year and Richard was thirty-two. Bessie had given up on either of them ever marrying and having children. At least that's what she'd said, time and time again, when they were all down in the basement grinding corn. Tilly didn't believe it. Bessie grieved so hard and long when they were gone. Tilly remembered her saying her life had been in vain. There would be no one to remember her or visit her grave when she was gone. That was when she'd told Bessie someday she'd have children and they could be her grandchildren. And she would always remember her.

She'd failed. She'd let the days go by. Good men had come and gone and she'd brushed off their proposals. Now it was too late. Bessie would never see grandchildren. Not even surrogate ones.

Tilly felt his presence without turning to see him towering over her. If she ignored him maybe he'd go away. She shut her eyes tightly and tried to conjure up a vision of Bessie rocking on the porch at the Morning Glory. It wouldn't appear. Couldn't get past the image of Ford in the attic and looking under the kitchen cabinets for a still.

He sat down beside her. Sparks jumped across the foot of space separating them. It didn't seem right with Bessie not even settled into the ground properly. Her soul should be grieving, somber and dead, not quaking with desire.

"I loved her," Tilly whispered.

"So did I. And I think the old girl liked me too. Remember, just last week she was throwing rocks at me?" Ford talked around an orange-sized lump in his throat.

"Your Irish is surfacing," she said.

"Does that sometimes. We're a maudlin lot when we love someone."

"Did you tell her?"

"No, but she knew."

"How?"

"She was a wise woman. She loved you and Clara and Tucker. When I first came to town I had a hard time figuring out how y'all and Bessie and Beulah were connected. Inez told me that they were fast friends with your grandmother. Bessie lost her sons and kind of adopted you three. Beulah lost her one daughter when she was a toddler and took on Katy's family too."

Tilly nodded, the failure of her place in the big picture weighing heavy on her shoulders.

Ford expected her to break. Thought for sure he'd have to soothe a grieving woman, send his best white shirt to the laundry when she finished crying on his shoulder. She surprised him. She stared off into space, the softest expression on her face. Even though her blue eyes were blank, he knew she was somewhere off in the past reliving experiences with Bessie. Perhaps her grandmother and Beulah were involved in some of the memories. She didn't share but didn't tell him to leave either. She didn't even acknowledge his presence, but sat beside him in a trance, giving him all the time he wanted to study her. He saw the hard, brittle woman he'd gone toe-to-toe with so many months melt away. Under the tough façade was a soft heart that loved and couldn't bear losing.

For more than an hour they sat in comfortable silence. She, in her mind, saying good-bye. He, lending support the only way he knew how, simply by being there. Finally she sighed; he reached across the space and laid his hand gently over hers.

Nothing had ever felt as right as his touch at that time. From somewhere far away she swore she could feel Bessie smile. A light breeze scooted through the cemetery, picking up leaves and scattering them across the graves. A small white cloud scampered across the blue sky. "Good-bye," she whispered as she let Bessie go. Peace flooded her heart.

"Want to walk back to town?" Ford asked.

"I think I'm ready," she answered.

He laced his fingers in hers, pulled her up and kept her hand in his. She lengthened her step just slightly, glad for the fuller skirt of her newest black suit. He shortened his, deliberately going slower, wishing they had to walk all the way to California. She tugged at his hand when they reached the Morning Glory and he followed her to the porch where she sat in the chair next to the one Bessie always chose.

"Sit with me." She untangled her fingers from his and pointed to the third chair.

He didn't realize how tense his muscles were until he melted his tall frame into the rocker and set it in motion.

"Tell me about Rayford Sloan," she said after a while.

"He's the sheriff."

"The star tells me that. What made him a sheriff? Where was he born? What does he intend to do with the rest of his life?"

"Why?"

"Because if you tell me about yourself, it'll take my mind off my own failures," she said honestly.

"I was born in Bogata, Texas, thirty-five years ago." He wondered what she'd failed at but didn't ask. "When I was sixteen I got into some trouble. Whiskey and the wrong crowd. My father should've taken a strap to me, but what he did was even worse. Put me to work for the sheriff in Bogata. Running errands. Sweeping the jail. Seeing those men and what breaking the law got them gave me a good education in what I didn't want. Straightened me up quicker than a trip to the wood shed."

"Your dad got the Indian in him?"

"No, Daddy was a full-blood Irish. Black Irish, they said, because he had dark hair and eyes. No red hair or blue eyes in this branch of the Sloans. Mother was half Indian. He found her up here in Oklahoma when it was still Indian Territory. Over around Tishomingo. Married her even though it wasn't acceptable. He loved her enough to tell society where it could spend eternity."

"Brothers and sisters?"

"One sister. Lives in Deport, Texas. Has a houseful of kids. Seven, last count. All boys. Married a rancher. Good thing. That many boys need a broad place to run and lots of chores to keep them out of mischief."

He was amazed how easy it was to open up to her as they sat on the porch that fall day. A brisk breeze shaking down the last of the leaves from the trees and bringing the promise of winter. The warmth of Bessie's memory still vivid in the other rocking chair as if she were listening in on their conversation.

"You think she knew the end was near?" Tilly touched the arm of the chair next to her.

"No, I don't. If she had, she would have said many good-byes. But I don't think she faced it with fear, either. If she awoke even one second before she stopped breathing, I expect she smiled at the trip ahead of her and jumped from this life into the next without fretting one bit. Bessie lived a long life and she wasn't afraid of anything, not even the end."

"I'm going to grow up and be like her," Tilly declared.

"Are you going to throw rocks at me?"

"I don't know, Ford. Throwing rocks means I like you. I don't know if I like you or not."

"That's a step up from the way we first started."

"I guess it is at that."

"Ready to go to Clara's? I can take you out there or home, either one in the sheriff's car."

"Not yet. I love Clara like a sister and Beulah almost as much as Bessie. But I'm not ready to smile and be in company just yet."

"Want to be alone?"

"No, I want you to tell me more. Tell me about what brought you to Healdton?"

"You did," he said honestly.

"Me?" She cut her eyes around at him, forgetting all about Bessie.

"Folks on the town council knew your grandmother ran 'shine. They also knew your mother was in on it and that Katy Anderson taught you the trade. They want the whole area cleaned up, legal-like. I have a reputation for doing that, Tilly. They sent me a letter. I came and talked to them. The old sheriff was ready to hang up his spurs. I guaranteed them I'd leave Healdton, Wirt, Hewitt, every bit of it, sparkling clean of moonshiners before I left. They said if I could put you out of business, everyone else would fold up out of fear."

Anger replaced mourning. Tomorrow morning she'd grind up twenty-five pounds of meal and start a fresh mash. In three weeks she'd be ready to deliver the first batch.

"So when are you leaving?" she asked through clenched teeth.

"You figure it's shiny clean, do you?"

"You found any stills?"

"Couple of small operations. Smashed one down by the creek last week. Tore up one the week before that. Not anything big enough to produce what goes through Lucky's place in a week, much less the local hotel and the one in Ardmore."

"You think you've put me out of business?"

"I'm not so sure you were ever in the business. Thought you were at first. Then I kind of figured you were leading me around by a nose ring because you were mad at me for putting you in jail. Inez kept the gossip going and was the center pin of the group who hired me. After her recent stunt, I'm not sure I was wise to believe her."

"So when are you leaving?" she asked again. It would be easier to take care of her customers if he was gone and yet the thought of him riding out of town on Akhil's back left a cold core in her chest.

"When I get another offer. You going to miss me?"

"I'll miss your horse." She didn't look at him. Didn't dare for fear he would see the pain in her eyes.

"Thought I might find you here," Tucker yelled from the street.

Neither Tilly nor Ford had even noticed the truck stopping out front.

"Looked at the cemetery. Clara is having a fit and Briar sent me to bring you home." Tucker's long legs made short work of the yard. He sunk into the third rocking chair and kept a steady rhythm, out of sync with the other two, but comforting to him after a long, mentally exhausting day.

"Ford is leaving. Taking another job as soon as he finds one," Tilly said bluntly.

"That's not a surprise. He agreed to stay until he cleaned up the area. Man said from the beginning he was a drifter. That upset you, Tilly?" Tucker asked.

"No," she lied. "He's a grown man. Can ride in when he wants. Ride out when he wants."

"I'd think you'd be glad to see him go," Tucker teased.

"Why's that?" Ford asked.

"You rub her wrong," Tucker said.

"And you don't?" Ford raised an eyebrow.

"Sure, I do. But I'm not a drifter. I'm a permanent fixture. She has to live with me. Come on out to the house with us. Might as well take advantage of Flora's cooking before you drift out of town."

"Thanks, I'd like that. Doubt if I'll be drifting much before Christmas."

"Good. Maybe you'll take a likin' to Flora's cookin' and stay around past that." Tucker stretched when he stood up.

Tilly wanted to kick the porch post when she passed it, but kept walking like a proper Southern lady right out in front of the two men who were discussing the price of a good bull. Bessie was buried. They could go on with life without any effort at all. *That's men folks for you, all right,* she thought. One minute Ford was tender and kind, the next talking about leaving Healdton before Christmas.

She sat in the middle. One big man–cousin on her left, driving, discussing farming and ranching. Big man–sheriff her right, his shoulder pressed against hers in the tight space. Listening. Making comments and asking questions. In the middle, wanting to wring both their necks, Tilly wondered exactly why Ford was a sheriff anyway. He talked and sounded like a rancher. Like Tucker.

They were still chatting about hay and how the winter could be so hard the farmers would run out, what with the drought and all, and the hay crop being so slim, when Tucker nosed the pickup into Briar's front yard. Libby ran down off the porch to wrap her little arms around Tilly's legs and hug her tightly.

"I was afraid they'd put you in that hole with Miss Bessie," she whispered.

"No, honey, only people who have died get buried." Tilly stooped to be on the same eye level with Libby. "Miss Bessie has gone on to heaven to visit her sons that died a long time ago. And to talk to my Granny and all her friends that went before her. I'm still here. I'm not going to die anytime soon."

"I hope not. Miss Beulah, she told me the same thing about Miss Bessie. I believe her. I do. But I believe you more. Come inside and see my new doll dresses that Momma made for me." Libby pulled her hand, leading her away from the men.

"You all right, Tilly?" Clara met them just inside the door.

"I'm fine." Tilly hugged her cousin tightly. The foyer smelled richly of fresh cut roses. The last ones of the season, those with the richest aroma. "Nice roses."

"Supposed to frost tonight. Really heavy frost. I cut every one of them. You sure everything is good?"

"I'm sure. Did you know Ford is leaving by Christmas probably? Says he came here to clean up the area and has decided they were full of bull anyway. Town council figured if they could put me out of business, then the rest of the area would fold far as moonshining went."

Clara led the way into the huge living room where Beulah rested on a deep, plush sofa, a pillow behind her head, her eyes closed, snoring loud enough to wake the folks more than twenty miles away in Ardmore.

"Momma, Tilly was going to come up to my room and see my dolly dresses you made me," Libby said.

"You go get them and bring them down here." Clara hugged Libby close to her side and then kept an eye on her as she skipped out of the room. "Been worried about her. She loved Bessie and this is her first death. Briar and I explained as best we could. Beulah told her Bessie had gone to heaven to visit her two sons that were already dead."

"She'll be all right. Don't worry about that one. She's smart and she'll take it all in stride. Better than us old dogs," Tilly said.

Briar peeked into the room and waved at Clara.

"We're going to the barn to see about the new colt. Send Libby when supper is ready," he said just above a whisper.

"You couldn't wake her with a dinner bell." Clara waved toward Beulah. "She's worn out both mentally and physically."

Briar disappeared and Clara went on, "I don't know how she's going to run the Morning Glory without Bessie. It took both of them to keep things going even with Dulcie's help."

"Don't underestimate Beulah. She could probably run the town and do a better job of it than the council they've got elected right now. To think they were asinine enough to think that if they put me out of business the whole place would run a close second to heaven itself. Men are going to drink. Women, too, if they've a mind to, and when they want a drink, they'll find it. It wouldn't have to be my liquor and it wouldn't have to be from my customers, either."

"I know that and you know that, but people often need someone to blame for their imperfect world," Clara said.

Tilly chewed on that thought for a long while, until Libby came skipping back into the room with a rag doll and a handful of clothing. So who was Tilly blaming for her imperfect world? Was she settling the fault on Rayford Sloan because he'd been so instrumental in causing her to shut down the stills? Or was she mature enough to realize her world was of her own making and whatever faults were at the core of it were her own?

"Aunt Tilly, were you listening to me?" Libby stamped her foot.

"No, I wasn't," Tilly said honestly. "But I am now. What did you say?"

Libby rolled her pretty eyes and shook her head hard enough that her dark curls bounced. "I asked when you and the sheriff were going to get married and have a baby so I could have a real live cousin to play with. One who didn't run off to Kentucky and never come back."

Clara giggled.

Beulah stopped snoring and sat straight up so she could hear the answer to that question.

Flora stopped mid-stride in the doorway.

"Why would you think the sheriff and I might get married?" Tilly sputtered.

"He looks at you like he could eat you right up. Like Daddy does Momma," Libby said.

"Out of the mouths of babes," Beulah yawned. "Libby, honey, come here and let me see those dolly dresses. I've got some scraps at the inn that might just make her another dress or two. Be good for me to have something to do this next week to keep my mind busy."

Tilly could have kissed Beulah. At least until she winked at her, letting her know the same question that had perplexed Libby had been on her mind.

Flora announced supper was on the table. Libby was sent to gather the three men into the house. Beulah went from the sofa to the kitchen sink where she washed her hands. She was the first one to sit down at the table and take stock of what Flora had prepared. A platter of thick-sliced ham. Whipped sweet potatoes topped with chopped pecans. Lettuce wilted with her own hot bacon dressing. Corn on the cob dripping with sweet cream butter. Tall glasses of iced tea. Hot rolls. Bessie would have loved it all, and she'd think of her good friend with every bite.

"So y'all hear the latest gossip?" Tucker said after Briar offered grace and bowls were being passed.

"No, and I can't believe you're about to tell us." Clara shot him a look down the long table.

"Why'd you say that?" he asked.

"Because you say gossip is for women and you wouldn't spread it for nothing," Tilly singsonged the words in a monotone. "Remember, women gossip and that's why you'll never use a woman lawyer or let a woman doctor touch you."

"That's right. That's the gospel according to Tucker Anderson. Women do gossip and that's where I heard this from. Women standing right beside me at the graveside service. Didn't know the old girls, but they know all about the Morning Glory and who lives there. Said that Cornelia was keeping company with George and pretty soon it would just be Nellie and Beulah in that big old inn."

"Cornelia and George?" Beulah's hand stopped in midair, sweet potatoes dripping from her fork back into her plate. "Great God in heaven. How did that happen?"

"Well, I guess she's been going in there after her school hours and they've been talking. He's asked her to take a drive this next Sunday after church," Tucker said.

Ford watched Tilly out of the corner of his eye. The news didn't faze her at all. She picked up a hot roll, buttered it and sipped her tea.

"And there's more if you're interested." Tucker enjoyed his role as messenger.

"Don't tell me Nellie is trying to beat her time." Beulah loaded her fork with potatoes again and made it to her mouth before Tucker sucked in a lungful of air so he could deliver the next tidbit.

"No, Nellie doesn't want George. At least that's what the two women said. Nellie, they say, is going to retire from teaching after this year and go to live with her sister. The two of them are going to run a boarding-house like you do," Tucker informed the whole group but he looked at Beulah. Might as well make her aware of the changes right around the corner.

"Well, I'll be damned," Beulah swore. "Pardon my language, Libby. That's a bad word only old women can say so don't you be letting me hear it come out of your mouth."

"Aunt Tilly's not old and she says it," Libby piped up. Ford chuckled.

"What are you laughing at?" Tilly reached around Tucker and slapped Ford on the shoulder. She wasn't prepared for the tingle in her fingers and drew her hand back quickly.

"She knows you pretty well," Ford said.

"She's a smart little girl." Tilly stuck her chin out.

Libby preened, wobbling her head from side to side.

"Before you two start bickering again I have one more thing to tell you. I swear that's the reason I don't want a woman. All they do is fight with you until they catch you and then make you miserable until you die. Can't see why George is wanting to replace Inez. You'd think he'd be glad to cut his losses and get on with a peaceful life," Tucker said.

"We were not bickering." Tilly narrowed her eyes at Tucker.

"And Tilly is not my woman." Ford set his jaw.

Briar dabbed the corners of his mouth with a snowy white napkin so he could cover the grin. Clara did the same. There were some things a couple had to figure out all on their own or else it would never work. Tucker had better learn to keep his mouth shut or run. Sitting between the two of them when they were both itching for a fight to cover up their real feelings wasn't a real smart place to be.

"Okay, okay." Tucker threw up his hands in mock defense.

"What's the other news? Olivia is leaving me too? I swear I'll have to train up a whole new lot of boarders the way things are going. You want to come live in my inn, Ford? Maybe I'll just rent to good-looking men from now on," Beulah said.

"I might but I'm probably going to leave by Christmas. Did my job here in town and it's time to look for another boomtown to get shaped up," he said.

"Oh, you think you've done your job, do you? Well, for your information, Your Highness, there's lots of moonshining going on right under you little nose. You couldn't catch a good 'shiner on a bet." Tilly leaned forward and looked around Tucker straight into Ford's dark eyes.

"Want to put money on it?" He narrowed his eyes until they were little more than slits with fire flashing from them.

"Hey, hey, you two stop fightin' or Momma will make you stand in the corner," Libby said loudly. "Uncle Tucker, is Olivia moving too?"

"If I can get these two children to behave, I'll tell you that story too," Tucker said with another chuckle. "I swear you two fight worse than we did when we were kids. You'd think you were brother and sister."

"If she'd been my sister I would have drowned her at birth," Ford said, only a slight tone of joking in his voice.

"Praise the Lord for not giving me a brother if he'd been like you," Tilly answered quickly. "He'd have never lived to see his wild teenage years. I'd have shot him and buried his sorry carcass under the lilac bush."

"I'm waiting to hear about Olivia," Beulah said loudly, putting an end to the argument.

"She's going to Ragtown for the Sunday afternoon service with Julius," Tucker said.

"Olivia?" Tilly couldn't believe her ears. "What about Danny?"

"Danny sent her a letter sayin' he was marryin' his teenage sweetheart down in Beaumont. She says that she's giving up her wild ways and settling down with Julius. Of course, he's got to think it's his idea but she's going to let him chase her until she catches him," Tucker said.

"I still can't believe you're spreading gossip." Clara's face was a picture of amazement.

"Just thought you ladies might like to think on something else other than a funeral. And besides, Bessie would have loved hearing all that," Tucker said.

"I don't think I've heard you talk so much in your whole life," Tilly said.

"Usually don't have anything to say and besides, most of the time I can't get a word in edgewise with you two women cousins yapping all the time," Tucker told her.

"Are you two going to fight now?" Libby asked.

Everyone at the table laughed.

After supper, Tucker drove Ford and Beulah back to town. Clara took Tilly home and waited until she got inside before she went back home to her husband and daughter. Life would go on, a bit of sadness creeping in now and then when she thought of Bessie, but the sun would come up the next morning. And that's the way Bessie would want it. She'd turn over in her grave and come back to haunt them if they didn't get on with living.

Tilly hung her dress in the armoire and slipped into a nightgown, sat down in a chair beside the window and watched the stars twinkling like diamonds in a bed of deep blue velvet. The day she'd dreaded was finished. Ford had helped her get through it all. His hand in hers. Even arguing at the supper table. She'd miss him when he was gone. He'd awakened a need in her for someone to call her own. Someone like Briar was to Clara. She wanted a marriage and children.

"When are you going to marry the sheriff?" Libby's sweet little voice echoed in her heart.

"Every path has a few puddles," she whispered as a lone tear ran down her right cheek. "Rayford Sloan is a puddle. I'll walk right through it but I won't look back. When he drifts out of town, I'll forget him," she told herself as she turned back the covers on her bed and slipped between the sheets.

Her heart didn't believe a word she'd said.

Chapter Eleven

Tilly's arms ached from grinding corn. Fifty pounds of cornmeal awaited the first step in starting a mash. She stared at the full buckets of fine yellow meal. In her anger she was more than ready to fire up the stills. However, her heart and soul just refused to think about doing all that again. She should sell the stills, but if she did, someone would know she'd been in the business and Ford would find out.

She backed up and sat down on the bottom step. Why should she care if he found out she'd sold a couple of stills? He couldn't prove they'd been used in years and years, not since her grandmother died. The realization that she cared what he thought of her came as a shock huge enough to make her heart race. They'd sparred. They'd kissed. They'd danced. All of it had been exhilarating. Being in his presence made her aware of every nerve in her body.

The rumble of a car drew her back into the present and sent her out of the basement in a hurry. She slung bales of hay over the doorway and slung open the barn door to find Ford not ten feet away, walking away from her, going toward the pasture where Akhil grazed. Think of the devil and he shall appear. Only she'd never realized until that moment that Lucifer didn't have to be wearing horns and sporting a spiked tail. He could be more than six feet tall, dark-haired, ebony-eyed, broad-shouldered, slim-hipped, and could walk with a swagger. He could entice her to sell her independence, her soul, and to lay her heart at his feet with one of his kisses.

"Good evening," she called out to him.

He turned at the sound of her voice. "What are you doing in that barn?"

"Checking on things." She shoved the door shut and went to meet him halfway. The last thing she needed was the devil hunting around in her basement.

"You keep your moonshine business in that one?" he teased.

"Of course. Would you like to search it?"

"I'm just teasing, Tilly. I've given up on owning that car of yours. Thought it might be nice to drive around in it a few weeks before I stripped off the radiator cover and sold it at public auction. That would show the whole area that I'd brought down the big Sweet Tilly 'shiner and they'd better go deep underground or else find some other way to make a living." Ford grinned.

Her heart flipped around in her chest, threatening to

pop a few buttons on the flannel shirt she wore. "So you aren't going to shadow me anymore?"

"Sure I am, just in case I'm wrong. Never have been in the past but there's a first time for everything," he said. Even in overalls a size too big, rolled up at the ankles, work boots and a faded flannel shirt, she took his breath away. In that moment, as they stood before each other, sparring again, he realized he didn't want to leave Healdton. For the first time in his life his wanderlust had been buried and he wanted to stay.

He couldn't. He had nothing to offer Tilly. Not one thing except a silver star pinned to his vest and a heart full of love. Neither was enough. Not for the lovely Matilda Jane Anderson. She deserved a man who'd made something out of his life. One who had land and cattle, or an oil company—anything. He had nothing of worth.

"Must be tough," she said.

"What?" The thunderbolt that had just rattled around in him had obliterated the line of conversation.

"Keeping that perfect halo shined and that set of wings all white and fluffy," she said.

"Why would you say that?" He rubbed his jaw.

"You said you'd never made a mistake. Only angels are that perfect," she told him.

He remembered. "Guess so," he mumbled. "I came to see Akhil. He's going to get fat and lazy."

"I expect he'll work it off when you leave. The sheriff's car doesn't go with you and you might have a long ride to wherever the next boomtown is or the next rowdy bunch of moonshiners need to be routed out."

"Never know." His chest constricted. She was ready for him to go. Ready to get rid of him and his horse. He was a day late and several dollars short, and he'd never wanted anything worse in his life.

"I'd join you but I've got to get dressed for the poetry reading tonight. It's a memorial for Bessie. We'll be either remembering something about her or reading a poem for her," Tilly said.

"Why would you do that?"

"Because those of us in the poetry club loved her. She came to the meetings for years. Up until about a year ago she never missed a one. She and Granny and Beulah. Mostly it was just to support me and Clara in our endeavor to be cultured."

"I see," he said. "Well, I'll not bother you. I'll just pet my horse and stay out of your way."

"Have fun." She crossed the grass, now brown after the recent frosts, and went inside where she shut the door and slid down the back of it, sitting on the floor. "What a mess," she mumbled as she removed her boots.

She got dressed in spurts. First shucking out of her overalls and shirt, peeping out the window at Ford having a one-sided conversation with his horse. Choosing a dress, and holding it next to her chest while she checked to see if Ford was still there. Slipping it over her head while he pulled up a handful of dried grass from the fence post and holding it out to Akhil. Brushing her hair. He ran his fingers through his too-long thick black hair, sweeping it away from his broad forehead. Rolling the back up into a bun at the nape of her neck so her hat would fit perfect. He rolled his head in a circular motion as if trying to work a kink from his neck. Cramming her feet into black kid leather slippers that matched her bright red dress with a black collar and cuffs. He kicked at a stone, sending it skittering across the yard.

When she picked up her purse and opened the front door he was opening the door to the sheriff's car. "That didn't take long." He stopped and took in the sight of her in long, lazy looks.

"If a woman can't get ready to go somewhere in thirty minutes or less, she shouldn't be going," Tilly said.

"Bessie, Katy, or Beulah?"

"All of them." She laughed. "But I could have said it."

"Could have. May in the future when you have a bunch of daughters. But that was wisdom of sages," he said.

"And I'm not a sage?"

"Not yet. How old are you, Tilly?"

"Thirty, and it's not polite to ask a woman her age. So you see I'm an old maid. Probably won't ever have a bunch of daughters."

"Oh, yes you will, darlin'. That's going to be your punishment for being so pretty. You'll have to pay for your raisin' with them."

"I'll take that as a compliment, Ford Sloan, and thank you for it. I've got to go or I'm going to be late."

"Everyone invited to this or is it a private poetry reading?" he asked, not wanting to let go. Not yet.

"It's public. Always has been." Shivers brought

goose bumps on her arms. She was glad she wore long sleeves and a crocheted shawl.

"Then, Miss Anderson, could I escort you there in the sheriff's car?"

"Are you asking me for a date?" she asked in amazement. Surely she'd heard him wrong.

"I guess I am at that." He nodded.

"Why? You're leaving. It could amount to nothing. Just a waste of your time."

"It's not a waste this evening. Yes, I will be gone, but that doesn't mean two adults can't enjoy spending a little time together. You are quite lovely, Miss Tilly. I would be honored to take you to the poetry reading and maybe a cup of coffee afterward at the hotel."

"Okay." One evening. Two adults. A little time. Poetry reading that bored him senseless. Sitting across from him in a hotel dining room pretending that the whole evening didn't matter. Why had she agreed?

No one said a word when they walked in together. Tilly docked it up to there being so many people there. Cornelia and Nellie. George. Julius. Olivia, who'd declared after the first time she attended that it was more boring than watching the second hand of a clock. Beulah. Tucker. Briar. Clara. Minerva, the clerk at the hotel. Three little gray-haired ladies dressed in black from her Sunday school class. Tilly finally remembered all their names. Cora. Esther. Naomi. Quite a group for a poetry reading that usually had barely a handful of people.

Clara called the meeting to order and read a poem about a young tree becoming an old tree and how the birds built nests in the branches. She likened the poem to Bessie in that she'd set her roots in Healdton as a young person and never left, making her home there so long that there were those who trusted her good advice like nests in the branches.

Beulah had a poem that said if you go first and I remain, to walk slowly so she could catch up. Tilly hated to admit it, but she feared Beulah wouldn't last long now that Bessie had already gone. When she finished the poem, she looked up at the ceiling. "And if your spirit can hear me, Bessie, you'd best not get in a hurry. Wait a spell. I'll be along."

There were few dry eyes in the place by the time Olivia took her place behind the podium. "I don't have a poem. I'm not real good with poetry and I don't understand it most of the time. But I did like what Clara said and what Beulah just read. I could understand that pretty well. Instead of a poem, I have a Bible verse. Matthew five, verse eight. 'Blessed are the pure in heart for they shall see God.' I think Bessie was very pure in heart and I think she's seen God by now. I just hope He realizes what a jewel he has."

"I'll be damned. Didn't think that girl had a brain in her head," Tilly whispered to Ford.

"Swearin' right after she's read from the Good Book. You'll be on your knees for hours tonight," he whispered back.

"I don't have a poem either." Julius took his turn. "I said everything at the funeral and you were all there so I'll just add my 'Amen' to Olivia's sentiment. I will say this. The Bible says there's a time for sorrow and a time for joy. Bessie wouldn't want us to be spending too much time on the sorrow, I wouldn't think."

Tilly made her way to the front of the group next. "I looked through my poetry books and couldn't find a thing. I did find an anonymous quotation that I liked and it seems fitting for my friend, Bessie. It went something like this. 'When we come to the edge of the light we know, and are about to step off into the darkness of the unknown, of this we can be sure: Either God will provide something solid to stand on or we will be taught to fly.' I was worried about Bessie going off in that darkness until my friend told me that she would have jumped from this life into the next with zeal. And I do believe that she is flying now."

My friend. Hal Ford didn't hear the sentiment but he picked up on those two words. He didn't want to be her friend. He wanted more.

When everyone had spoken, refreshments were served. Tilly found a spot behind an enormous ivy plant and watched from afar. Cornelius and George paired off, talking in low tones. They actually made a better pair than George and Inez ever did. Cornelius wasn't a beauty but she had a good head on her shoulders. George was balding, wore thick glasses, and no doubt at one time thought he was a lucky man to have someone like Inez. Tilly had never seen the two of them with their heads together discussing a poem in a book Cornelius had open. Not once had she heard Inez do anything but belittle George. Things turned out the way they should. Someone said that once, but she couldn't remember if it was a great scholar or her grandmother.

She sipped her punch and craved coffee. Libby sat in Beulah's lap. From the hand movements, Tilly figured they were discussing doll clothing. Beulah told her about some kind of fabric and Libby's eyes glittered. Surely a child like that would keep Beulah from chasing down the path to eternity to catch up with Bessie. Libby needed a grandmother. Beulah needed a granddaughter. Hopefully, that would keep her from lying down and giving up on life.

It was true about Olivia and Julius. That girl had done a hundred and eighty degree turnaround in the last few weeks. The twinkle was gone from her eyes. She even walked with less bounce. It was sad. Julius should have appreciated her for the lively young woman she was rather than making a stereotyped preacher's wife out of such lovely material.

"Who are you hiding from? I saw you come in with Ford. Were you with him or did you just arrive at the same time?" Clara asked.

Tilly jerked and had to jump back a step to keep from spilling punch on her dress. "Where did you come from? I'm hiding."

"Snuck up on you." Clara laughed.

"You sure did. I came with Ford. A date of sorts. He came out to the farm to see about Akhil and asked me if he could escort me to the reading and buy me a cup of coffee afterward."

"A date?" Clara exclaimed.

"Of sorts. Just one time. He's leaving in a few weeks. Just two adults enjoying each other's company," Tilly explained.

"You two enjoying each other's company. Now that's a joke. Maybe enjoying each other, but all you do is argue," Clara answered.

"Why do you suppose that's the way of it? When did you and Briar stop fighting and start loving each other?"

"We fought as long as the conflict kept our hearts in turmoil. When we gave up and admitted that we were in love and let our hearts have their ways, then we stopped fighting. But let me tell you a secret. I still sometimes start a rousting good fight just so we can go up to the bedroom and make up," Clara whispered conspiratorially.

"Then I guess we don't have a chance. Both of us have hearts as hard as diamonds and as stubborn as Tucker's old one-eyed mule."

"You do at that. You in love with him?"

"If I was I wouldn't admit it to anyone. Not even myself so I suppose we're in for another few weeks of disagreements."

Ford looked across the room and caught her eye about that time. He would have put Akhil on the auction block to know what those two women were discussing. He tilted his head toward the door. A silent question asking if she was ready to leave. She nodded slightly.

They slipped out the door without much ado and walked two blocks to the hotel. He slipped the shawl from her shoulders and pulled a chair out for her. She ordered black coffee and he did the same.

"So tell me about Matilda Jane Anderson. I know

you were named for two old mules your grandmother had when she was selling moonshine. What else is there?" He stirred his coffee to cool it.

"Matilda and Jane were my great grandmother's mules. Every time one got too old to pull the wagon, they got another one and kept the same names. I'm not so sure it was a good idea to name me for mules. It may be what caused the stubborn streak." She sipped the coffee.

"A rare woman. One who admits she's stubborn." He grinned.

Her heart melted into a puddle somewhere around the toes of her shoes. The sound of his voice. His smile. Why did she have to fall for a man she couldn't have? One who sure wouldn't want her, a former 'shine runner, and the most outspoken woman in all Carter County. When Ford settled down he'd want a woman like Olivia had become. One willing to walk two steps behind him.

Obey.

That word wasn't in Tilly's vocabulary. She might find a man she could live with someday but she'd die a withered up old maid before she obeyed any one of them.

"So you going to tell me about yourself or not?" he asked.

"You've lived in town long enough to know the history of the Andersons. Granny was Indian. Grandpa was English. A crusty old fellow, I've been told. He was dead before I was born. Bessie and Beulah said there wasn't a woman around who'd have him and his temper. But Katy Evening Star Anderson tamed him down right well. She owned the ranch so Grandpa got that when he married her. He didn't have as much as she did but Granny said he had two hardworking hands. She also never doubted for a minute that he loved her. That meant a lot. They had three boys. He was a good father. She was an excellent mother."

"That's telling me about your family, not you," he said.

"Got to know the past to understand the present and see the future," she said.

"Bessie, Beulah, or Katy?"

"Me. That's straight from the mule's mouth." She looked across the table deep into his dark eyes. She could swim in those waters for the rest of her life and take the essence of them with her through eternity.

"Okay, then, tell me more." He settled into his chair, propped his elbows on the table and his chin on laced fingers.

"Tucker's dad was the oldest. When he married, Granny bought him the farm next to hers. My aunt loved her so much she insisted the farm be named for her. That's why it's called Evening Star and the brand is a star. Grandpa said Granny's name fit her because the evening star was the brightest in the whole sky."

"I thought he was a crusty old fellow. Sounds like a poet to me."

"Talk to anyone in town and they'll tell you my grandpa was meaner than a constipated rattlesnake . . ."

Ford threw back his head and laughed so hard tears came to his eyes. "I can't believe you said that."

"What, that he was mean? Well, he damn sure was."

"No. Constipated. I didn't think ladies said that word."

"Ladies probably don't. Haven't you noticed, you are not keeping company with a lady. I'm Matilda Jane Anderson, named for a couple of mules and you know what trait they are famous for, other than stubbornness."

"Good Lord, Tilly."

"Not that I inherited that problem. At least not on cookies and coffee." She laughed with him.

"Okay. Okay. You were saying the neighbors thought he was a blister but your grandmother brought out the poet in him?"

"That's right," Tilly told him. "Anyway, my parents went to Houston for a holiday when I was thirteen. The big hurricane that wiped the place off the map took them with it. Granny finished raising me and Grandpa didn't have the market on crusty. She was wise but I didn't get away with a lot."

"Did you try?"

"I'm sure I tested her patience many times a day."

"So she taught you to farm, raise cattle, and what else?"

"You still looking to trip me up with the moonshine idea?"

"Maybe."

"Won't work because I'm smarter than you are, lawman. She had her fingers in lots of pies, Ford. A little gold mine in California that still produces a nice little sum every year. Some real estate in New York. There's a man in Dallas who takes care of the business. I go see him once a year and he goes over the whole package with me."

"So you are the richest woman in the county like they say?" The words were like a stick beating against his hollow heart. The farm alone was enough to toss him out of the running. She'd just mentioned many other ventures that would brand him a gold digger if he did ever admit his newly found feelings.

"No, I'm not. Clara is."

"You mean Briar is. He's the one with the oil wells."

"Briar has a lot of money and assets. Clara has ten times as much. Her father was in banking. Granny set him up there because a woman couldn't run a bank and she needed a bank in Healdton. She sent him to Philadelphia to learn about the business. He met Clara's mother there. An only child. Guess it 'bout caused a war when they eloped. There he was, part Indian and she was one of the hoity-toity easterners. Her parents disowned her. Never spoke to her again. But they never got around to putting it on paper, so when they died one winter she inherited the whole pie. She wouldn't touch the money. Put it in a trust fund for Clara."

"But why did she run a boardinghouse if she was that rich?"

"Because she wanted to."

"Is that why you run a farm?"

"That's right. What would Clara have done with nothing to do? She would have really gone crazy."

"I can't see you going crazy if you didn't have a farm to run." He toyed with his empty cup.

"Don't guess I would, but I like it. I enjoy the plowing. The decisions. All of it."

"Cleaning?"

"Hate it."

"So now I know a couple of things about you. You admit you're stubborn. You don't like to clean, and you are not the richest woman in Carter County."

"Me in a nutshell." She held up her empty cup. "Coffee is gone. Guess the date is finished."

"Not until I drive you home. Tell me what you'd be doing if everything you had suddenly disappeared." He draped the shawl around her shoulders, left a bill on the table, and kept his hand on the small of her back as they left.

Tiny little sweat beads formed between her breasts and ran down the cleavage like a miniature river. What had generated such heat when the outside air was so cool with fall settling in around them like a wool cape?

"What did you say?" she asked when she was settled into the front seat of the car.

"I asked what you'd do if you found yourself penniless."

"Why, I guess I'd run for sheriff. You are leaving and it looks like the town is going to need one," she smarted off.

"Good enough." He laughed again. He couldn't remember the last time he'd enjoyed an evening so much. Or ached so badly for another one just like it. He took a long hard look at the months he'd been in Healdton and realized all the good memories had Tilly tied up in them. "You really think you could be a sheriff? Take care of killings? Run down 'shiners? Make people uphold the law?"

"Just because I'm not a man doesn't mean I don't have a brain. Women can do most anything a man can do. You can see it in the bigger cities even now. Men folks going off to war. Women staying home and keeping the home fires burning but also building war machines in the factories. Doing what used to be only men's work because there are no men to do the jobs."

"So you could do the job then?"

"Honey, I could take care of my farm, do your job, and raise a whole house full of kids."

"Why aren't you raising kids now?"

"Main reason is that society frowns upon a woman raising a house full of kids when there's no husband involved. Now a man can run around like a tomcat, testing every sand box he comes to and no one says a word, but you let a woman do such a thing and they'll string her up even if it is modern day nineteen-seventeen."

"So you'd like kids but you don't want a husband?"

"Don't know that I don't want one. Just haven't found one I'd have."

His ego deflated. She'd found him and evidently wouldn't have him.

"Want to come in and continue this enlightening discussion?" she asked when he parked and helped her out of the car.

"No, ma'am. I think I've had enough for one night, but Momma taught me that a gentleman always walks his date to the door." He looped her arm through his.

"What else did Momma teach you? That good little

lawmen always kept company with good girls. Never a thirty-year-old woman destined to become an old maid? Steer clear of anyone who has even the taint of moonshining in their past?"

"She taught me to say, 'Yes, ma'am' and 'No, sir' and not to judge a woman by her age or looks. I don't think we ever had a set down talk about moonshining. If Daddy drank he kept it in the barn and never mentioned it because she would have sent him packing. Her father didn't hold his liquor too well from what I've heard. Ended up dead because he was drunk when he was trying to break a horse. So she didn't teach me much in that area, other than by example. I told you I tried whiskey and wild crowds once. It got me a long job of mopping the jailhouse floors."

"Good Momma you got there." Tilly opened the front door.

"Tilly?" Ford laid a hand on her shoulder.

She turned back to find him closer than she'd imagined. So close she could see his eyes echoing her own desires. Before she could say a word, he'd drawn her into his arms. The kiss sent quivering tingles up and down her arms and spine but she could have no more broken away from it than she could have sprouted wings and flown right up to heaven with Bessie. She leaned into it, flicking her tongue out to taste the chill of the evening and cold coffee on his lips. Her arms came up instinctively around his neck and her fingers, having a mind of their own, tangled into the dark hair he wore slightly too long. Beat for fast beat, her heart matched his.

"Old maids do not kiss like that," he whispered when he pulled away from the embrace.

"How would you know?" she shot right back, glad he couldn't see the high color filling her cheeks.

"Momma taught me not to kiss and tell," he threw over his shoulder as he walked off the porch.

"I'd like to meet your Momma. Bring her to Sunday dinner," Tilly yelled as he crawled into the car.

He just waved, letting her have the last word. There was no way he'd bring his momma to meet Tilly Anderson. That would be like taking a drunk man to Lucky's. Rayford's Momma had been shoving every woman within a fifty-mile radius of Bogata, Texas, in his pathway since he turned twenty-one. Tilly would be the same as waving a red flag in front of a bull. She was outspoken, which was exactly what his Momma said he needed. No wimpy woman to be whining in the kitchen with her on holidays. Tilly would step right up and voice her opinion on anything whether it agreed with his, Momma's, or even God's. If he and Tilly did marry and produced children and they looked like Tilly, Momma could show off her grandchildren, preferably granddaughters, with pride. Everything Momma would want right there in one package named after two old mules that had pulled a moonshiner's wagon. Even at that, Momma wouldn't bat an eye at accepting Tilly. Ford could feel the acceptance in his heart. Everything Ford needed, and the woman had just informed him she didn't want a husband.

Tilly made her quaking legs carry her in the house

but she leaned against the window frame as she watched him leave. Why, oh why had he ever come to town? Now she'd measure every other man by the yardstick called Rayford Sloan and no one would ever come up to the mark. Lord Almighty, but that man could raise her hackles and then plaster them down slick with kisses that made her knees go to jelly. How was she ever going to live without him? And yet, she most surely couldn't live with him. He'd never forgive her for outsmarting him with the moonshine.

"You don't kiss and tell?" she said aloud. "Does that mean I don't have to tell either? If he can kiss old maids in his past and not tell, can I have made moonshine and not tell? I'll have to think about that. When my legs will take me upstairs. I'd just about sign over the Sweet Tilly to him for another one of those kisses." She slid down to the floor and leaned against the wall.

Men! Blast them all to hell on a rusty poker. No, not men in general. She'd dealt with them for years. It was one in particular who had set her world at a strange tilt and she couldn't get it back on the right rotation around the sun.

Chapter Twelve

Frost lay on the ground like a thick frosting on a light chocolate cake that morning. Ford left footprints across the yard to the porch where he'd knocked on the door to let Tilly know he was on the place checking on Akhil. No answer there so there were more prints around the house to the back door where he knocked heavily again. Nothing met him but a wary old tomcat peeking out around the side of the house before it disappeared. Disturbed frost out to her car where he laid his hand on the hood. Cold. She hadn't been anywhere that morning. Must still be out doing chores.

He started to the barn where they'd stored hay but noticed small boot prints leading to the small barn nearest the house. The one he'd seen her coming out of the evening he'd taken her to the poetry reading. The one he'd never been inside before. The door was slightly open so he slipped inside and looked around. A very small building with a few bales of hay. Perhaps where she brought a horse when it was ready to foal. Or a calf that was having troubles surviving. He sat down on a bale of hay and studied the place even more. No stalls to keep livestock inside. Weathered gray wood. What on earth had they built the barn for and why was it still standing? It didn't even have the smell of horses or cows.

He was on his feet and leaving when he noticed a sliver of light shining between two boards on the north wall. Hay bales were askew in that area where they were stacked neatly in the rest of the building. He leaned toward the boards, expecting to find that he would be looking straight out into the yard when he peered between them. Instead he found a wooden handle. It wasn't boards he stared at but a door. He looked up. The peaked roof line left no room for an attic so the doorway must lead down.

Tilly sat with one leg on each side of a narrow bench in front of a corn sheller, feeding full, dried cobs into the machinery, the kernels filling the wooden bin. As she finished, she tossed each cob behind her into another bin. She'd been using the machinery so long it was second nature. The first time she'd shelled corn she was so short Katy had to put a pillow on the bench to raise her up high enough to see what she was doing. The next step, if she was really going back into the business, would be putting the kernels through a grinder. She had fifty pounds of cornmeal waiting but hadn't decided whether or not to light the fires under the stills. Her hands were busy with work she'd done so long she could accomplish it with no thought, so she let her mind wander. Ford and his passionate kisses. Would she ever find someone else to make her blood boil? Did he feel the same way?

Ford put his hand on the door handle and held it there for several minutes, listening to the steady rhythm of something below him. The slight vibration in the floor. The vague noise that told him there was a cellar beneath the barn. The perfect place for a moonshine business. His extra senses went into overtime as he cautiously opened the door and inhaled, expecting to fill his nostrils with the bitter aroma of sour mash. Nothing wafted up the narrow staircase except light and a faint fog of dust. His heart constricted with what ifs wrapping cords around it so tight he could scarcely breathe. What if Tilly did have a 'shine business down in the cellar? Perfect place but where was the water? She had to have water to make moonshine. That's why they found so many stills beside riverbanks or near creeks. What if he had to make the decision to file charges against her? What if he found a booming operation and couldn't take her in? What if he had to make the choice between taking her down or giving up his job and self-respect?

He took the first step inside the constricted confines of the staircase, feeling the need to squeeze his shoulders inward. If he turned around right then he'd never know, but the unknown was the scariest thing in the world. He made it halfway down, yellow light and pale dust mixing together in the room at the bottom like the haze of smoke in a pool hall.

Tilly hummed "Shine On Harvest Moon." A new song by Nora Bayes. By the time harvest came around again Ford would be long gone, leaving only his memory engraved on her heart and the warmth of his kisses on her lips. She made up her mind while she hummed that she was finished with moonshining. Yes, she could produce a quality stump liquor and get paid top dollar for it, but she didn't need the money. And she was tired of giving up the time for it. She'd rather make doll clothes for Libby's new rag doll or maybe even learn to keep a decent house. She'd grind her corn for the pigs and chickens. She'd make a sour mash from some of what she'd already made into cornmeal, and use the rest for cornbread. She hummed louder. Once the decision was made and could be written in stone, she found peace in it.

Ford took two more steps and heard someone humming away. It sounded like that new Nora Bayes song. The one he'd played on Tilly's Victrola record machine. By the time he reached the bottom and found a whole moonshine business before him, he wished he'd never set foot in the barn. Why couldn't he have just gone on to check on Akhil and leave well enough alone? A water well occupied the middle of the room. So that's where the water came from . . . how convenient.

Tilly felt his presence and for several seconds thought it was because she'd been thinking about him. She finished taking the corn from the cob and tossed it behind her, the thump telling her that she'd hit something other than the wooden box where she'd thrown cobs for the past hour. Her whole body did a knee-jerk when she turned around and found him standing behind her.

"Looks like I found you," he said hoarsely.

"Guess you did." She nodded.

"Looks like a real operation down here. Water. Stills. Cornmeal."

"Yep, it was a big one in its day."

"Come on, Tilly. I caught you. Fess up."

"To what? You caught me removing corn from the cob. You caught me with fifty pounds of cornmeal in a bin that I plan to add water to for the hogs. They like that when the weather is cold. You caught me humming. Which one of those things is against the law, Sheriff Sloan?"

"Tilly, those are stills. Old ones but damn good ones. You probably made sixty quarts a week down here, hidden away from everyone."

"I believe Granny Anderson said she could make eighty on a good week."

"Don't evade the issue," he growled.

"Don't see things that aren't there." She tried to ignore nervous sweat beads forming on her neck. "Open up the stills. Take a look inside. Run your little tongue around them if you must. There's no liquor in there, Ford. You see any mash in those crocks? How about jars of 'shine? Feel any fires? Smell any mash?"

"Why is all this equipment still down here if it hasn't been used in years?"

"I'm smart enough to do your job, lawman, but somehow I don't think I'm big enough to haul those stills or vats up the stairs. I'm not sure how Granny got them down here, but she had to have had some big muscle help. And what am I supposed to do with them once they're up there?"

It sounded plausible. The only thing in the basement was cornmeal and one woman who was as cool as the frost he'd just waded through. He opened the first still and inhaled deeply. Not even the faintest whiff of moonshine. Nothing but clean air. Dust on the top of everything like it really hadn't been used in years.

Tilly held her breath until her chest hurt. Thank goodness for a heavy coating of corn dust all over everything. And a healthy dose of cleaner made with lye soap and vinegar to clean the stills. Dead or alive, Granny would expect that. If they'd been left with the slightest trace of brew in them to mildew, she would have turned over in her grave and haunted Tilly the rest of her life.

"Why didn't you come clean about this at the very first? Why did you have me running circles around myself?" He crossed his arms over his chest and tilted his chin back, looking down his nose at her.

"Sure. Sheriff Sloan, darlin', I've got a whole operation down in the cellar under one of my barns. It's got stills, vats, a corn grinder, even a well tapped into an underground well. Come on over and I'll show it all to you. I'm sure you'll think it's all been sitting there for years since you want my car and farm on the auction block for your own personal gain."

"That beats letting me think you had that car outfitted for running 'shine," he snapped.

"Don't you take that tone with me, lawman! Don't you dare. You're the one who's come barging in on me while I was doing my winter chores. Corn takes a lot less space to store if it's taken off the cob and any farmer worth his salt knows that." She found herself fitting into the role of the victim rather than the crook easier by the minute.

He wanted to believe. Honestly, wanted with all his heart.

"So you going to get Tucker and Briar, maybe George and a couple of Briar's heavy duty oil men to come down here and haul all this out or are you going to leave my heritage alone?"

"Tilly, will you give me your word of honor you won't make moonshine down here? I figure you know how or at least have the basic knowledge since your grandmother did."

"Got a Bible you want me to swear on? Why don't you go grab Julius and get him to witness before God and all the golden courts of heaven? Leave my stuff alone, Ford. Trust me."

"Can I trust you?"

"What did those kisses mean to you?"

"You are evading the issue." He uncrossed his arms and ran his fingers through his hair.

"Tell you what. I'll leave the door at the top of the stairs wide open. I won't drag bales of hay over to cover it ever again. You can stop by any time you want and check on the operation down here. And while you are here feel free to grind some corn into meal or use the machinery here to take it off the cob. I'd appreciate the help."

"You are serious." He looked her in the eye.

She didn't blink or look away.

"I'm serious," she told him.

"Good. Now, I'm going to see Akhil. He'll think I've forsaken him. This evening Beulah has invited me to supper at the Morning Glory. Dulcie is cooking a turkey with dressing. Must be something important going on," Ford said.

"Must be because she's invited me too. Clara, Briar, and Libby are coming too. Wonder if she's telling us she's selling the Morning Glory." Tilly was glad to change the subject.

"Tilly, I'm going to keep a check on this just to keep you honest," Ford said as he started back up into the barn.

"Be sure to shell some corn while you're down here. Good hard work might keep you honest too." Getting control of her racing heart wasn't an easy thing to do, but she picked up another ear of corn and went to work, making herself hum again. If she could run 'shine right under his nose, she could very well keep her wits about her until he was gone. She had all day to give in to a case of nerves.

Ford left the door open and sat on a bale of hay. The noise of her work and humming filled the small barn. The absolutely perfect setup and yet she wasn't using it. Hadn't been in a while because there was dust on everything. The stills, vats, and crocks were all dry as bone. Even the well had a cover on it, but still something didn't seem just right. He'd bet his boots and his badge that she'd made 'shine sometime in the past. She'd kept her cool but there was a little niggling voice inside his head that kept saying he'd been right all along about that car. The Sweet Tilly car with the big metal plate on the radiator and no seats in the back. He'd eat his boots and badge if it wasn't outfitted with heavy duty shocks as well. No one would outfit a car like that without a reason.

He left the barn and made two trips around the car, looking in the windows and checking out the plate on the front again. He dropped down on his knees and then laid flat out on the cold earth to check under the car. Sure enough, heavy duty suspension. Now why would she do all that? When she ordered the car special made, she didn't even know Rayford Sloan was coming to town so she didn't do it just to rile him. The sheriff who'd kept the law for twenty years hadn't decided to retire when Tilly bought the car. If she'd wanted to remember those mules and the saying on her grandmother's wagon, she could have had *Sweet Tilly* painted on the side of the door.

"Still trying to sniff out some 'shine? I might have a jar left in the house from back when Granny was running it if you've got a mind to have some whiskey and run with a wild crowd," she whispered so close to his ear that he bumped his head on the bottom of the passenger door when he jumped.

"It'd kill me if you've had it that long," he brushed his trousers off when he stood.

"That might be the idea. Give it up, Sloan. I'm running a farm here not 'shine all over the county. I don't kiss like an old maid but I'm fast becoming one. You've got a horse to see. I've got work to do. Beulah asked me to bring the pecan pies for supper. I'll see you there. Give Akhil an extra hug for me. I saw him yesterday but haven't been down to that pasture today. He says I can ride him next week."

"You stay away from my horse." He pointed his forefinger at her.

"Oh, I thought I'd ride him over to Ragtown and deliver a saddlebag full of liquor to Lucky's. Maybe I'll tell your deputy about it before I go and make it real easy for him to catch me. Then he'll own your horse and can sell him at auction to the highest bidder," she taunted.

He glared at her and wordlessly stormed away, the set of his shoulders and tilt of his chin leaving no doubt that he was angry.

She opened the back door, kicked off her boots and went straight for a chair. Anything to support her weak knees. That man did have a way of affecting her that way. It made her as angry as he was when he couldn't prove she'd been selling illegal booze for years. She could have easily wrung his neck and enjoyed watching his pretty brown eyes bug out as he died.

What was it Clara had said? Something about when she and Briar got over being so upset inside themselves and let their hearts guide them, it was then that they knew they were in love?

Chapter Thirteen

Everyone gathered around the dining room table at the Morning Glory Inn at six o'clock that evening. The sun was nothing more than a sliver of orange on the horizon so Beulah had candles scattered up and down the table in no particular order. A brass stick here, a crystal one there, one made from a chunk of driftwood. Dulcie brought turkey nestled down in a bed of cornbread dressing to the table. The male conversation about horses over in the corner of the dining room came to an abrupt halt.

"Dulcie, will you marry me?" Ford asked.

"Oh, pshaw, man. Old woman like me might be able to cook but I couldn't keep up with the likes of a good-lookin' man like you. Best go lookin' at someone else at the table tonight, not this old lady."

Beulah took her place at the head of the table and issued orders about who sat where. When everyone

211

was seated there was an empty seat right beside Olivia. Clara and Tilly both looked at it as if the devil filled the place.

"You two can blink now," Beulah said. "That's a place for Julius. He's invited tonight, too, but he got a call out to the Roberts's house. Granny Roberts is dying again. I swear that woman's been on her deathbed once a week for twenty years."

"Beulah!" Clara exclaimed.

"Truth is truth. Cover it in chocolate and it's still truth same as if you sink it down in the middle of a cow patty," Beulah said. "Since Julius is going to be late, Tucker you ask the grace on this table tonight."

Tucker kept it brief, thanking the Lord for the day, the food, good friends, and asking His blessing on all of it.

"Amen," Julius said from the doorway. "Got here as soon as I could. Granny Roberts had a near death experience, but she's recovered and having potato soup for supper. Is this seat mine?"

"Yes, it is." Olivia patted the chair beside her.

"How many times has she been about to draw her last breath since you got here? Briar, you pass that turkey this way. I had Dulcie go ahead and carve it up in the kitchen so it would be less trouble," Beulah said.

"I've been here about seven months. I quit counting after the first fifteen. She just wants attention and everyone is too busy to give it to her," Julius said.

"Hmmpph." Beulah's shoulders shook with the expression.

"Before we all get started, I suppose you're wondering what this occasion is all about." Julius turned to smile at Olivia. "Beulah wanted to do something nice for us. This is our engagement supper. I've asked Olivia to marry me and she's said yes. We'll be married in two weeks at the church. The judge is coming through for Joe's trial that week. We thought we'd have him do the ceremony after church on Sunday afternoon. Beulah has offered to have a reception here at the Morning Glory for us afterward. We'll have a little honeymoon and be back by Wednesday night services."

The bottom fell out of Tilly's appetite. Everyone else was smiling and telling Olivia and Julius how happy they were so no one noticed the fake smile on her face. No one except Ford, who couldn't figure out why Tilly wasn't cackling like the rest of the hens in the room. After all, another good man was about to bite the dust. Olivia had caught the preacher. Who'd have ever thought it. Ford had stopped Danny on more than one occasion on his way home from Ragtown with Olivia in the car with him. More than once, Ford had searched the car for illegal booze. Looked to him like Tilly should have been happy as a little piglet in a fresh wallow that her friend was going to settle down with a respectable preacher man.

While the women cleared the table after the meal was finished, the men drifted into the living room with their coffee. Talk went to the winter ahead, crops, the new church going up in Wirt, whether Joe would be found guilty or if the jury would believe that he was acting in self-defense and how Red was the best danged checker player in the whole county.

In the kitchen, where the women gathered around the table with their cups of coffee, conversation centered on the wedding. Olivia was subdued. Clara, ecstatic about planning a reception, and insisting Olivia let her pay for the whole thing. Dulcie and Beulah declaring that they could do the cooking. After all, they had just two weeks to plan and prepare and it would keep them busy. Olivia's parents wouldn't be able to come until the day of the wedding, and besides, they should enjoy the day with Olivia, not be strapped down with cooking and entertaining.

"Tilly?" Olivia looked across the table.

"Yes?"

"You haven't said much, but I would like to ask you and Clara both to stand up with me, be my bridesmaids. I guess Clara would be a matron of honor, though, since she's married."

"Thank you, but—"

"We'll be glad to. We're honored. Let's all three go shopping for dresses tomorrow." Clara shot Tilly a look meant to straighten her up. "What color do you want us to wear?"

"I love red but I suppose that's out since I'm marrying Julius. How about Christmas green, and we could arrange some poinsettias to decorate the church? Do you think they'd be pretty in a bouquet?"

"Green is good," Clara said. "This time of year I bet

we could find matching dresses like that. And white for you. Would you let us buy your wedding dress for you?"

"Oh, I couldn't. You've done so much already. Tilly saved my life and made me realize I needed to make some changes," Olivia blushed.

"Hells bells, Olivia, don't go making me a hero! I didn't save your life because I was worried about you. You could've done the same thing I did if you'd stopped whining and thought about the situation. Red's not very big and he was drunk."

"Good Lord, Matilda Jane, who burnt your oatmeal this morning?" Dulcie shook her finger at Tilly. "You ain't been nothing but a wet blanket. Here Olivia is, settling down with Julius and not some fly-by-night oil man and you're not even happy for her."

"No, I'm not," Tilly said.

"Why?" Olivia tilted her head to one side.

"Because Julius sucks all the life out of you. You came to town and went to work at the bank. All independent and you didn't give a royal damn what anyone in this town thought about you. You even dated Danny, the best-looking and wildest one in the crowd. Just stuck up your chin and dared everyone to cross you. Then Danny sends you a heartbreaker of a letter. Red takes you hostage and you become someone else. I just don't like it that you've changed. Be yourself. Be Olivia."

Silence was so heavy that it could have been cut out in great chunks.

"This is Olivia," she finally said.

Tilly shook her head and started to speak.

"No," Olivia held up her hand. "This is Olivia. I mean it. When I first came to Healdton and rented a room here, I was living in a rebellion bubble. My parents were determined I'd marry a man from Ringling back when I was sixteen. Kind of an Inez story. I told them I'd run away and never come back if they didn't put a stop to it. My first taste of rebellion. A few years went by and I didn't show any more signs of rebellion but I was almost twenty and they were ashamed of me. An old maid. Then I heard about the teller job and I came over here and got it. They were really ashamed then. Their daughter working out in the public. But I did it."

"And you found yourself." Tilly nodded.

"No, I didn't, Tilly. I didn't find myself. I ran from myself. I didn't like that quiet woman I really was. I wanted to be more like you, but in doing so, I lost me. I went out with Danny. I flirted with Briar before you married him, Clara. I flirted with Tucker. I was searching for someone like Julius."

"Sure you were," Tilly argued.

"No, I really was. He makes me feel special. Like I'm the only woman in the whole world. Like he'd shrivel up and die if anything happened to me. He's not rich like Briar or even good-looking like Ford or Tucker. But when he kisses me, I swear it's like I hear the bells of heaven ringing. I just hope I'm good enough for him. That I can make a preacher's wife."

"Really. You're not just saying those things?" Tilly asked.

"I'm so serious it scares the devil out of me." Olivia giggled for the first time.

"Then, hells bells, girl, let's go shopping tomorrow. And the last time I looked, things were pretty shabby in that parsonage so maybe we'll do some shopping in that area while we're at it." Tilly jumped up and hugged Olivia.

"I can't believe you're using that kind of language in front of the preacher's wife," Dulcie said.

Olivia just laughed harder. "I wouldn't change Tilly for anything. Anymore than I could change me."

"I still can't believe it." Tilly sipped her coffee.

"Believe it." Olivia patted her shoulder. "And thank you for all you've offered to do for me and Julius."

"You? Quiet and happy? That is a pretty big thing to try to picture in my head," Clara said.

"Sometimes a woman just spreads her wings and tries on a new life. It was fun but when I was in that house with Red and he was drunk, I found out that I didn't like it as well as I thought I did. It's tough to change a tiger's stripes. I'm ready for quiet and happy and I'm sure ready for more than just a few kisses from that preacher in there." Olivia's eyes twinkled.

"You saying that a woman goes back to what she was all along when she gets ready to settle down?" Tilly asked.

"Guess so. If you ever get quiet and docile or start wearing little pink housedresses to church, I'll start worrying about you," Olivia said.

"Lord, I'll just arrange for the undertaker." Clara giggled.

"I'm always going to be full of sass and vinegar?" Tilly asked.

"I hope so," Olivia said.

Ford looked across the checkerboard at Tilly. She appeared to be studying the next move, her hand on a red wooden disk, but her mind was off somewhere between earth and the clouds. The engagement party broke up before eight and she seemed restless so he'd asked if she'd like to come to the jail for a game or two. Now he wondered just what those women had talked about in the kitchen. How to broach the subject again of the stills in her basement and the offer to take them away for her? What she'd say if he told her he'd had an offer from Deport, Texas, not very far from Bogata where his parents lived?

"So what do you want in a wife when and if you ever settle down? Do you want a little mouse that stays in the corner, who walks two steps behind you and keeps your shirts ironed?"

"What brought that on?" he stuttered.

"Olivia and Julius," she answered honestly. "I'm still having trouble seeing such a marriage. She's been wild and free. Flirting with everything that wore pants."

"Did she flirt with you? You wear overalls pretty often." He grinned.

"You know what I'm talking about," she snapped.

"She didn't flirt with me. I'm hurt to the bone." He threw his hand over his heart.

"I'm worried about her," Tilly said.

"Don't be. She's a big girl. She's over twenty-one and so is Julius. They'll be all right."

"How do you know?"

"Because he loves her."

"I bet they said that about Inez and George too."

"Probably."

"Why would she choose him? He's the very thing she was running away from when she came from Healdton. She didn't want a staid, quiet life. She wanted adventure."

"She didn't choose him, Tilly. Choice is not a matter in love. Chance is. There's an adage that says, 'No one falls in love by choice, it's by chance. No one stays in love by chance, it's by work. No one falls out of love by chance, it's by choice.' Think on that for a while. Inez wasn't willing for the work anymore so she made the choice to fall out of love. I think Olivia will work at the marriage. Everyone has to, Tilly. My parents had their fights. Still do. But they work at it. My sister loves her husband and believe me, there's times when he has to work at it rather than make the choice to fall out of love."

"You really believe that?"

"I do. You asked what I want in a woman. My mother says I need someone with a good strong backbone to argue with me and keep me on my toes. She says that I'd soon tire of a mealy-mouthed little mouse of a thing."

"I'm not asking what your mother thinks." Tilly's big blue eyes pierced his soul.

"You proposing?"

"Hells bells! No! I'm just trying to figure out what it is men want. Julius needs a woman to help him in the ministry and Olivia is willing to do that. But it's hard to fathom, isn't it?"

"Yes, but not impossible."

"I'll just have to hope for the best. I want her to be happy." Tilly jumped three of his checkers and put him in a place where there was no way but to concede defeat. "There's another old adage I like. 'Life is simpler when you plow around the stump.' Guess I was trying to plow through it. Thanks for the game, Ford, and for listening to me ramble again."

"Quite welcome." He nodded. "I'll walk you to your car."

He brushed back his hair and settled a black felt hat on his head. "Something I want to talk to you about. Without an audience?"

Red chuckled. "Been layin' here listenin' to you two sashay around love talk all evenin'. Looks like anything you got to say can't be worse than what we already listened to."

Joe guffawed. "You better plow around that big old sheriff stump, little lady, and get on with your life. Don't be wastin' time with him. I'll be outta here in a couple of weeks and I like women full of spit and vinegar. You wait for me and I'll show you just how special you are."

Both Ford and Tilly turned crimson. Neither of them answered the two prisoners they'd thought were sleeping in their cells.

"What have you got to say?" Tilly asked when they

reached the Morning Glory where she had parked the Sweet Tilly.

"I've been thinking about those stills. It bothers me that they're on your property. Just having them there could cause a lot of trouble with the next sheriff. I think they should be removed. Thought I'd get Tucker and Briar to help me get them out of there. I didn't want to mention it in the jail just in case Red or Joe was awake. Glad I didn't."

"Thank you, but no thank you. What's down in that basement is part of my inheritance, Ford. I don't want it destroyed. I don't want it moved. It's been there for more decades than we've both been on this earth. I'll just leave it there."

"Next sheriff might demand where I'm offering." He reached out and brushed a strand of hair away from her face.

The electricity generated in his touch caused her knees to go weak, but she was used to that reaction. God knew how much she'd miss the excitement when Ford was gone. And God only knew. She'd never be able to explain it to another soul. Not even Olivia with her newfound love mentioned jolts of raw passion tearing at her heart.

"Next sheriff can figure out things on his own. Could be he'll be dumb as a box of rocks and I'll start up the stills and make a killing on 'shine again." She opened the car door and slid behind the wheel.

"Again? So you did make it?"

"Sure, I helped Granny lots of times before she died. I've done it all, Ford. Planted corn. Hoed the weeds. Harvested it. Shucked it. Shelled it. Ground it. Made it into mash. Even helped make worms out of copper tubing. Granny said if it wasn't produced from start to finish on Anderson land, it didn't belong in her quart jars. That bother you?"

"No, as long as it's in the past. Just thought I'd offer." He shut the door and leaned in the window. "Be careful driving home. Never know when a revenuer might be out looking and they'd spot this car a mile away."

"Why do you keep worrying with that old bone? I thought we'd buried it." She wrapped her arm around his neck and kissed him soundly on the lips. Sparks lit up the inside of the car like fireworks on the Fourth of July.

"Whew," he gasped when she pulled away.

"Take that home and think about it when you go to sleep," she said sassily as she pushed him out the window and rolled it up.

He was still grinning when the taillights disappeared. When he got back to the jail he sat outside in the chilly night air for a long time. He liked that woman. Really liked her. For the first time he truly wished that he'd settled down and accumulated something other than a pretty horse in his thirty-plus years. Something he could offer a woman like Tilly Anderson.

"Good Lord, I've gone and fallen in love with her!" The grin disappeared. He jerked his head around, scanning the town, up and down the street, inside the windows of the jail to see if anyone had heard him other than the Good Lord, Himself. "Now isn't that a damn pickle of a revelation," he mumbled.

I'll have to work at falling out of love, he thought, then listened to make sure he hadn't said that in his out-loud voice too. He shook his head violently, thinking that surely he could dislodge such a silly notion. It didn't work. *I'll be moving. Can't stay in these circumstances and can't do a damn thing about it if I did stay. Painful either way, but I'll start tomorrow putting out some feelers for a new place.*

Tilly slipped between cool sheets and warmed up a spot with her body heat, which felt steamy all the way home after that spontaneous kiss. That hadn't been too smart. Kissing Ford on the spur of the moment just because he was so sexy and turned her insides into a quivering mass of pure nerves. Sure, it had gotten her a dose of instant gratification, but now she couldn't sleep.

Crazy how things were working out in her world. Six months ago Clara was an eccentric old maid who ran a boardinghouse and went downtown every day at the same time to sit on the bench in front of the drugstore. Now she was happily married to Briar and had hit the gold mine when she married him because she got Libby in the deal. Bessie, who thought Clara, Tucker, and Tilly belonged to her and Beulah after Katy died, was dead. Olivia was getting married in two weeks to the preacher. Now that was still a shocker even if what she said had the ring of truth to it. What was it Beulah said? Truth was truth. Didn't matter if you hid it in a cow pile or a chunk of chocolate.

"Now I'm hungry," Tilly moaned. She pushed the

covers away and made her way downstairs. "That's what I get for not eating my fill of turkey and dressing. It's Julius and Olivia's fault. They could have waited until after supper to announce their engagement."

Knowing where everything in the house had been located her entire life kept her from needing a light. She padded across the foyer, the dining room, and into the kitchen. She went to the cabinet and took out a loaf of bread, found a jar of strawberry jam and was about to make a sandwich when she stepped on the slug, squishing it up between all five toes.

"Yuk!" she screamed loudly, stumbling around on her heel, trying to find the cord to bring light into the room. She groped and it evaded her. She danced around without setting her entire foot down, using words that would have scalded the hair right out of Julius's ears. By the time she found the string and gave it a hard pull, the devil himself would have been blushing at her language.

She sat down in the middle of the floor and looked at the three-inch slimy worm embedded between all her toes. No way was she touching that mess. Using a chair to hoist herself up, she hobbled to the sink, threw her leg over the edge and turned on the water. It took several minutes before the slug's remains were washed down the drain, another five before she finished scrubbing the residue away with one soaping after another.

"This is Olivia's fault too," she declared as she dried her foot, still shivering at the idea of what it felt like to step on such a thing. "If I'd eaten supper, I wouldn't be hungry. If I hadn't kissed Ford so brazenly, I wouldn't be awake. If I hadn't fallen in love with him, I wouldn't have kissed him. Hells bells, fallen in love with him . . ." She was taken aback at the concept.

She forgot all about the sandwich and sat down in the middle of the kitchen floor, carefully checking around for another slug. She knew she'd begun to care too much about him, but to actually admit she was in love took her breath away. When people stop fighting what their hearts know and admit they are in love. . . . Clara's words came back to haunt her.

"I can't. Not Ford Sloan. I just can't," she whispered as she dropped her head onto her drawn-up knees. "Not by choice but by chance. That's what he said. I still can't. I won't take that chance."

Chapter Fourteen

Tilly strolled slowly down the aisle. It had been years since she'd been a bridesmaid. Several of her peers married young at sixteen and seventeen and she'd been asked to stand with them. Others waited until they were nineteen and twenty, on the verge of being old maids, and she'd served several of them. Thirty-year-old women weren't brides or bridesmaids. They were old maids, with heavy emphasis on the *old*.

Tilly took her place beside Clara. Cornelia struck the right chords on the piano and the whole congregation stood, watching Olivia come down the aisle on her father's arm. A tall, lanky man with a hawk-like nose and thin nondescript hair. Her mother, Edna, looked more like Olivia. Twinkling eyes. Slightly graying hair. Tilly had liked her immediately. She was reserving opinion of Mr. Traversty for a while.

Instead of looking at the bride she glanced at the

groom. Julius glowed. Literally glimmered as Olivia came closer and closer to him. It was as if there was no one else in the church but he and his bride. Their eyes locked and held and their smiles reassured each other that they were right where they wanted to be that evening.

She let her eyes slide farther to George who wasn't paying any attention to the bride in her white lace dress and matching veil. His interest lay behind Tilly where Cornelia played the piano. He winked and Tilly noted a very slight slip in the wedding song.

Ford was on the other side of George. She stared at his boots. Polished so shiny she could see the reflection of the light coming through the stained glass windows. Little red and yellow patterns right there on his feet. Upward her gaze went. Trousers of his three-piece suit fit his legs and hips without bagging or sagging. Vest and suit coat both covered a broad expanse of chest and arms big enough to handle a bale of hay as if it were nothing more than air. Hair worn long enough to entice a woman to sink her fingertips into it; use it to pull his mouth down to wallow in a kiss so long it would make her knees quake. By the time she reached his eyes, she found them staring right back at her.

He smiled ever so slightly and she looked away. Lord, why was it so damned hot in the church? A blue norther flustered about outside but Tilly wished she'd brought a hanky to wipe her forehead.

"Julius, repeat after me," the judge said.

Tilly wondered how they'd gotten to that point

without her hearing a word of the ceremony. Surely she hadn't spent all that time gawking at Ford. Great God, she wasn't a sixth grader with pigtails who couldn't take her eyes from some little boy. She was a fully responsible woman on the verge of being an eccentric old maid.

Julius repeated his vows, not missing a word, looking right at Olivia.

How sweet, Tilly thought. She hoped Olivia never looked back and regretted her decision to settle down with a preacher. If she ever did what Inez had done, Julius would be devastated.

"And now, Olivia, repeat after me," the judge turned to her.

She didn't stutter or stammer one time. Spoke right up, loud enough that even old Grandpa Bannett in the back row heard her just fine.

Tilly sincerely hoped that Olivia would be happy in her new position.

The judge pronounced them man and wife and Julius laid a kiss on Olivia that came close to making Tilly blush. Maybe she'd underestimated the preacher if he could kiss that passionately in front of a whole congregation and God to boot.

Julius and Olivia swept out of the church as if they were walking on a puff of air. George offered Clara his arm and they followed right behind the bride and groom. Ford bent his elbow and Tilly looped her arm through it. The church got hotter. Not even the cold north wind blustering about cooled her down. She couldn't imagine why Olivia was shivering and Julius was warming her by drawing her closer to his side as they got inside the Sweet Tilly and drove toward the Morning Glory where they'd greet all their guests.

"Come on Tilly." Clara dragged her away from Ford's arm. "Excuse us, Ford, but we've got to hurry to the inn to help Beulah and Dulcie with last-minute details. You can ride with Briar and Libby."

"Yes, ma'am." Ford nodded. He'd never been a groomsman before and it was a whole new experience. His sister had eloped with her sweetheart and although he'd been to several weddings in his life, he'd never been asked to be a part of the wedding party. He remembered the wedding a few months before when Briar's sister married and there'd been dancing until late at night. He'd watched Tilly that evening from a distance, knowing she was a moonshiner and wishing she wasn't so he could ask her to dance.

By the time he and Briar arrived at the reception it was in full swing. People milling about, wishing the bride and groom a long and happy life. The wedding cake, a three-tiered white frothy concoction from Dulcie's kitchen, was cut right after Ford opened the front door. The line formed at both the dessert table as well as the one holding so many different covered dishes that just looking made Ford's mouth water.

He located Tilly serving punch and desserts from behind a long table draped with a white tablecloth. She smiled and his heart melted. He wished he could hear what she was saying to Olivia's mother, but the noise of so many people talking at once kept their conversation private.

Tilly handed Edna a cup of punch and the lady stepped around the table to speak to Tilly as she worked. "I want to thank you personally for everything you've done to make this day so special for Olivia. I can't begin to tell you how glad I am that she's found herself again. She's back to where she was before we made a bad choice for her. Her father was so angry when she left home to work in the public that he swore he'd never help her at all and he's been honor bound to keep his word. I do think he's regretted it."

"Maybe they can have a good relationship now," Tilly said graciously. "And you are very welcome to what we've done. Seems like we adopted Olivia when she came to live at the Morning Glory."

"Well, you've had such good success with the way she's turning out, would you like to take on four more? We have five girls. Olivia is the oldest. That would be Mary over there in the peach-colored dress. Margaret, beside her in yellow. Rachel, in the pale blue and Naomi in the lilac. Got any more preachers you could pull out of the woodwork for them?" Edna teased.

"The Morning Glory has produced several miracles in the past few months. Clara met her husband, Briar, right here. Now Olivia and Julius. Don't think I'd better press its luck," Tilly said.

"I can see why Olivia likes you. You're what she thought she wanted to be. But you just can't change a leopard's spots. She made a full circle and came back to what she was raised to be. A good girl."

"Let's hope she's a happy woman."

"That's the truth," Edna raised her crystal cup. "Thank you again. I must go talk to Beulah."

Tilly looked up at the next person in line to find Ford with only the width of the table between them. "Enjoying yourself, Sheriff Sloan?" she asked.

"Yes, ma'am. Nothing like a good wedding. Brings out the pretty and the good in everyone. Makes for a pleasant evening, doesn't it? Want to dance?"

"No music, darlin'. Beulah wouldn't take too well to us going up to her bedroom and turning up the volume to her Victrola, either. If God didn't strike us dead for dancing at the preacher's wedding, she would."

"Beulah has a Victrola?" He was amazed.

"Oh, yes. She and Bessie loved the new music. They'd go up there every evening and crochet on their altar cloth and other things for the church but they'd have their music playing and their toes tapping the whole time. Better move on down the line, Sheriff. Folks are getting impatient behind you, and besides, talking to a moonshiner will ruin your reputation."

"Admitting it or bragging?" He grinned.

"Just taking care of your good name," she sassed back. Great God in heaven, did he bring heat with him.

"Thank you, ma'am." He nodded and joined Briar and Tucker in the corner. They were talking about things that he could relate to. Hay lasting through the winter. Keeping help at the oil wells. But his ears and his eyes couldn't agree. Ears really wanted to listen and pay attention. Eyes wanted to drink in the sight of the woman he loved. Wanted to watch every nuance and aura surrounding her. Had to make memories that would have to last a lifetime because he could never admit his feelings.

"Pretty, ain't she?" Briar asked when Tucker went back to the food table for another helping of barbecued pork chops.

"Who?"

"That woman you're looking at."

"Tilly?"

"I was in the same place you're in so I know the look."

"No, Briar, you weren't. You had an oil company and something to offer. I've worked my whole life and all I've got to show for it is this badge."

Clara joined them before Briar could answer. "Darlin', come and meet Olivia's father. He's warming up to the folks a little. I know you can make him feel welcome."

Ford meandered out to the porch where he claimed a rocking chair. Three women behind him were talking about how the town's doctor was leaving town in a month. Right before Christmas. They'd heard that Magnolia Oil was bringing a doctor into Healdton. Of course his first responsibility would be to the oil company employees but Magnolia Oil had already put out the word the doctor could offer his services to the townsfolk, also.

Ford chuckled. That ought to get them a few more leases.

"What's so funny?" Tucker pulled up a chair close to Briar.

"Just overheard a conversation that Magnolia Oil is bringing in a doctor. You going to feel honor bound to lease your land to them since they're being so gracious to the community?"

"Hell, no. I wouldn't even sell to Briar and he's kin now. There'll be some that do, though," Tucker said.

"Politics. Every job has a bit of it," Ford told him.

"All except mine. I'm a farmer. Do what I want, when I want. Don't want to ever be anything else."

"Think you'll ever marry?"

"Times like this make us bachelors wonder, don't it? I'd love to have a wife and a family, but women these days aren't like they were when my Momma was alive." Tucker sighed.

"Times are changing. It won't be five years before women will have voting rights. That's just the first step. The war has speeded things up for them. Men off fighting. Women going to work in the factories."

"Guess I've had my head in the sand," Tucker said.

"You're head is always in the sand," Tilly joined them, sitting on the arm of the rocking chair beside her cousin and ruffling his dark hair. "We keep you in the dark. You couldn't take the shock. Way you always go around saying that you won't have a female doctor or lawyer in your sights. The bride is all ready to leave now. So get a handful of rice to toss at them for good luck."

"Nice of you to let them use the Sweet Tilly," Ford said.

"I've been thinking about buying a car for the church," she said. "Not as fancy as the Sweet Tilly but maybe a good used one. Olivia needs something to get around in and if Grandma Roberts ever does meet up with the grim reaper, Julius will need to get out there quickly."

"Thought you were dead set against that. If I remember right you made some comment about how if women were on the planning board at the church, you'd vote against it," Tucker reminded her.

"Women have the right to change their minds," Tilly said.

"Want me to take you home tonight in the sheriff's car?" Ford asked.

"No sense in that. I've got my truck. I'll drop her by," Tucker said.

"Thanks, you sweet little cousin." Tilly wanted to tie a noose in a good long length of rope and hang him from the nearest pecan tree. "I'll be a while because it's my job to help clean up. Since you'll be waiting for me, we can use an extra set of hands to put things right."

"Ahh, man," Tucker snarled. "You sure know how to ruin a good evening."

"Sure you don't want me to take you home? I'll be up late anyway," Ford offered again.

"No, I wouldn't deprive Tucker of helping wash dishes for anything. Thanks for the offer, though. Feels like it could snow. Why are you out here anyway? Hiding from Olivia's sisters?" she teased.

"Mercy, no!" Tucker exclaimed. "Olivia is the oldest and I'd have been robbing the cradle to look at her sideways. The rest of them are way too young for this old man."

"Someone will come along one of these days. She'll drift into town and turn your world upside down, Tucker Anderson." Tilly crossed her arms across her chest to keep the cold out, but one look at Ford and she was tingling with warmth from the inside out.

"Ain't marryin' no drifter and I'm not interested in anyone who'll turn my world upside down. If I ever marry, it'll be some sweet thing who knows her place," Tucker declared.

"We'll see," Tilly disappeared into the house to pass around a big crystal bowl of rice so everyone could take a handful. She suppressed a grin at the idea of the newlyweds going on their honeymoon in a car outrigged for a moonshining business. Ignorance surely was bliss.

Ford played a game of checkers with Red. The jury declared Joe not guilty and he wasted no time getting himself a train ticket from Ardmore to south Texas. The man he'd killed in self-defense did have friends and relatives in the area.

"Miss Joe?" Ford asked.

"Little bit."

"The year will be over before you know it. I've got a job offer over in Deport, close to my family. Not even a boomtown. No murders every week. Just keeping the peace in a sleepy little county," Ford confided in the prisoner.

"You'll go crazy." Red moved a checker into place.

"Probably, but I'm going crazy here."

"Tilly Anderson could do that to a man."

"Suppose I'll give my two weeks' notice at the council meeting tomorrow night. I'll recommend they hire Sam Wilson. He's been a good deputy. Think you can abide his checker games?"

"Reckon so. Told Tilly yet?"

"Haven't got a chance. Wanted to take her home but Tucker stepped in and offered. Couldn't very well insist without it looking like I was courtin' her."

"Why ain't you?"

"Red, I don't have a thing to offer. Few bucks in the bank over in Bogata. Not enough for someone like Tilly."

"Got over that moonshine idea, did you?"

"I think Inez was spreading malicious gossip." Ford moved a checker and ended the game on a victory note.

"Well, good luck. I'll miss you." Red stretched out on the cot and shut his eyes.

Tilly draped her dress over the back of a chair in her bedroom, removed her shoes and stretched her aching toes. She'd been up and going since before dawn and it was well past midnight. By now Olivia and Julius were in their room at the Hotel Ardmore. She wished she was in one of those fancy rooms with Ford.

"Hells bells, where did that come from?" she almost shouted. Was she never going to have a moment's peace until she told him how she felt?

She pulled the bedspread back and eased her tired muscles between the sheets. If she was this tired, she hated to think about how exhausted Dulcie and Beulah must be at their age. They'd put on a party though that Healdton wouldn't soon forget.

She sighed deeply and shut her eyes. When sleep finally came she dreamed of Ford standing beside Tucker at another wedding. Tucker was the groom. The bride was tall, not as pretty as she'd figure a woman would have to be to win Tucker's heart, but had the most beautiful green eyes. Ford looked over at her, bridesmaid again, and winked boldly. When she shook her head at him, he brought his hand up to his lips and blew her a kiss.

She awoke touching her mouth. It was still dark outside. The clock downstairs chimed three times and her body said it had not rested nearly long enough. "Crazy dream. He's leaving. I'm staying. He's just a drifter who's wormed his way into my heart and besides, Tucker is too damned cantankerous to get married." She beat a soft spot into her pillow and went back to sleep, only to dream the same thing all over again.

Chapter Fifteen

There were two things Tilly hated. Good-byes were both of them. She braced a cold wind already blowing bits of sleet to go to the barn where Akhil waited in a warm stall. She'd never pushed her luck and ridden the big black monster of a horse, but he represented Ford and all that she could never have.

"This is it, old boy." She pulled two apples from the pocket of her heavy wool work coat and fed him. "We've got a new sheriff in town as of this morning. Off with the old and on with the new, as they say. I'll miss you." Her voice broke and tears flowed so fast and furious that her cheeks were wet in seconds. Brushing them away was a useless gesture.

"Take care of him," she sobbed and ran back to the house.

One down and one to go. As difficult as it was to tell a horse good-bye, she couldn't fathom the pain in

238

telling Ford the same thing. She wouldn't do it. She didn't have to. In spite of the weather she'd go to Ardmore. Have lunch at the Hotel Ardmore. Shop for a new winter dress for Sunday. Maybe buy something pretty for the house or new music. Anything to run from another good-bye.

"Never run from a problem," Granny Anderson's voice came loudly through her conscience.

"What a Christmas present. This is supposed to be a happy time of year, not heart-wrenching," she mumbled as she hung her coat on the hook beside the backdoor and removed her work boots. In her bedroom she changed from her work clothes, overalls and a flannel shirt, into a midnight blue wool skirt, a heavy sweater of a lighter shade and shoes and socks. The outside was warm enough. The cold core inside Tilly Anderson couldn't be heated up. There wasn't a quilt thick enough or enough wood in the whole county to build a fire big enough to remove the ice covering her heart.

When he knocked on the door she was listening to music. She opened the door and motioned for him to come in out of the cold. "Akhil is ready," she said, not trusting her voice to say any more.

"I want to thank you for keeping him all fall and winter," he said stiffly. "I'm glad Tucker offered his truck and trailer to get him over to Ardmore to the rail station. It would have been a cold twenty-three miles for both of us."

She faced the glowing blazes and simply nodded. She didn't need to look at Ford. Everything about him was etched into her memory where she'd keep and cherish it forever. *So this is what it feels like,* she thought, as she held her hands out to take the chill from them. *This is what Clara felt like when that preacher ran away and never returned. This is what those beaus I had when I was young felt like when I spurned their advances. This is what rejection feels like. Painful as hell and I hate it.*

"Well, then good-bye, Matilda Jane Anderson." He longed to take her in his arms and declare exactly how he felt, but he simply could not. He had nothing and he wouldn't have the gossips saying he'd married her for her money and farm.

"Good-bye, Rayford Sloan," she said softly, keeping her back to him.

He dragged his heavy heart out the door, across the yard and to the barn. Akhil nuzzled his hands and followed him out into the cold weather. Ford eased him into the horse trailer and took a final look around at Tilly's place. What he saw was a cemetery instead of a farm. A place to bury his heart because it was sure enough refusing to go with him. Akhil was ready to go. Ford's body could go anywhere there was a job. But his heart wasn't taking one step off that farm. Not when Tilly lived there.

"Too bad," he mumbled. He started up the truck engine and kept his eyes straight ahead, not looking back at the lady in the upstairs window wiping her eyes on the curtain.

His trunk was already loaded. His horse getting a nice ride in the bad weather. He'd pick up Tucker at his farm and they'd talk about the weather and livestock all the way to Ardmore. He'd put Akhil in a special car, find himself a seat in the passenger part of the train and he'd put his feet under his mother's supper table that night. One step at a time. In a few weeks maybe he could grow another heart.

Tucker saw him coming down the lane flanked on both sides with bare pecan trees and ran out to jump inside the truck. "Didn't want you to have to get out in the weather," he explained. "Told you we were going to have a bad winter. Just hope there's enough hay in the barns to get us through it."

"Hope so," Ford nodded.

Tilly had never been a weepy, clingy woman in her entire life. She'd had no trouble standing up and telling the world just what she believed. She'd never really needed a thing that she hadn't found a way to get. The longer she stood sobbing at the window, the less she liked the woman in her skin.

"Can't do it. Even if he tells me I'm crazy, I can't let him go without telling him exactly how I feel," she declared aloud. "Shouldn't have let him take Akhil out of the barn. Now I'll have to chase him down, but hey, he's driving an old truck and I've got a perfectly good moonshiner's car out there." She talked as she grabbed her coat and ran outside to fire up the Sweet Tilly.

She met them at the end of the lane and honked, sticking her hand out the window at the same time and motioning for them to pull over. "Stop that truck or I'll follow your sorry rear end all the way to Ardmore and drag you home by your hair," she yelled.

They didn't hear her but Tucker waved. "Wonder what she's doing out on a day like this? Guess she's going into town to finish up her Christmas shopping. I swear, Libby is going to have the biggest Christmas morning of her life. Clara told Tilly last week if she bought one more present to put under the tree, she was going to ban her from the house. Tilly laughed and told me she was keeping several at her house until the morning we open presents together."

"Day after tomorrow." Ford checked the rearview. There was that big metal plate announcing to the whole world that Sweet Tilly was on the road.

"Yep, you'll be home in time for the holiday," Tucker said.

"Guess so. Wonder what she keeps waving her hand out the window for? She's going to freeze with that window rolled down. Think she's wanting us to stop?"

"Could be. Pull over. If we don't she'll pass us and wait in the middle of the road," Tucker said.

Ford found a wide spot in the road and pulled over. The Sweet Tilly came to a skidding stop right behind it. Ford slung the door open only to find Tilly already stomping toward him. The set of her jaw and the fire in her eyes told him he was in for a cussing and for the life of him he couldn't figure out what he'd done wrong.

"Tilly?" He crossed his arms over his chest.

"Ford?" She stopped two feet from him.

"Got a problem?"

"Big one."

"Need Tucker for something?"

"No, don't need Tucker. He can't fix it."

Ford frowned. "Then what is it? I've got a train to catch and we're having to go slow with the trailer."

"I've fallen in love with you," she said honestly.

"I know that."

"What are you going to do about it?"

"Not one thing. Can't do anything about it. I love you, Tilly, but that's not enough."

"Why?"

"Don't have a thing to offer you. All I own in this world is Akhil and what's in that trunk in the back of the truck. I love you and it kills me to leave you but . . ."

"Lot of pride there, lawman," she smiled.

His heart jumped back into his chest and began beating again.

"Guess so, but that's part of me too. Can't get rid of it."

"Life's easier when we plow around the stump," she reminded him.

"What are you saying, Tilly?"

"Guess since you got too much pride and I've just swallowed all mine, what I'm saying is I love you, Rayford Sloan, and I want to marry you. I've got a farm and a lot of other financial assets. They don't mean a damn without you to share them with me. You've got what's in that trunk and a horse. That's enough for me. Marry me."

"That's pretty brazen. Women don't propose. Men do."

"Guess so. This woman did because you can't."

"I can propose. Will you marry me, Tilly? Would you leave all this behind to live in two rooms above a noisy jail and be a sheriff's wife?"

She didn't even hesitate a second. "Yes, I will. Want me to go just as I am? I only have the clothes on my back but I'll leave the Sweet Tilly on the side of the road and crawl in that truck with you and Tucker right now and go with you."

Neither of them had moved a step but Ford did then. In two long strides he took her in his arms and tipped her chin back with his fist. "I love you. If you can swallow your pride and leave everything, I can swallow mine and bring nothing into the marriage but a heart that adores you."

She wrapped her arms around his neck, grabbed a handful of thick hair and pulled his lips down to hers. "Let's go into town and get married right now."

"Now? You don't want a wedding? My mother could come and my sister. We could do it up right in the spring. Clara and Libby, the whole town attending." He sunk his face into her hair.

"No, not in the spring. It's cold, Ford. I want a husband to keep me warm all winter. Right now! Tucker and Olivia can witness for us. Tucker can bring Akhil back home and we'll lock the gate at the front of the lane. I don't want a wedding. Planned one and had a wonderful time with it last month. I want a husband and a honeymoon in our home," she whispered.

"Why?"

She leaned back. Her blue eyes glistened as she looked into his dark ones. "Because I want you, Ford.

I want to wake up with you next to me. I want to be your wife. Living with me won't be easy. I don't want to give you time to change your mind."

By mid-morning, Akhil was back in his stall in the barn. Tucker had gone home and locked the gate on his way. Julius and Olivia were on their way to Ardmore to register a brand-new marriage license at the courthouse.

Tilly sat down on the sofa in the living room and took off her shoes and stockings, put on a record and held her hand out to Ford. "Could I have this dance?" she asked.

"Yes, ma'am." He gathered her into his arms. "People will talk. They'll say I married you for your money."

"Never cared much for gossip. Don't reckon I'll start caring now. I know why you married me, Ford. That's all that matters." She leaned into him. The floor was cold on her bare feet but she didn't even feel the chill.

After the song ended, he kept her hand in his and led her toward the stairs. "I've got one question, Mrs. Tilly Sloan. Did you run 'shine after I came to town?"

"Did you marry me just to get the Sweet Tilly? Seems you said you'd own it before you finished your job in Healdton." she asked.

"Did you marry me just to get Akhil?" he teased as he picked her up and started up to the bedroom.

"No, I married you to find some peace in my life. I was miserable without you. Could be I'll be miserable with you." She nuzzled the side of his neck.

"Probably. Can't see two hard heads like ours never arguing. But, darlin', I didn't marry you for the Sweet Tilly. It's just a car. The real sweet Tilly is right here in my arms. Now answer the first question." He kicked open the door with his foot and carried her over the threshold before he set her down beside the bed.

"Wrong room. My bedroom is across the hall." She laced her fingers in his.

"Any reason this can't be our room?"

"Not a one."

"Good. New room for a new couple. You going to answer my question now?"

She began unbuttoning his shirt slowly, taking her time, letting her hands roam over his broad chest, deliberately torturing him. "Tell you what. You answer a question for me. The last one of the day since I've got other things on my mind and I'll truthfully answer yours about the moonshine business."

"Anything you want to ask, I'll be glad to answer." He grinned. Finally, he would know for sure whether he'd been right.

"How many women have you been with?" She raised her head and kept her eyes glued to his.

The grin faded. "That's unfair."

"Some things are best left in the past. Forgiven. Forgotten. Not known. Right, darlin'?"

"Right darlin'," he agreed.

He kissed her, erasing even the idea of moonshining from his mind. He picked her up and laid her gently on the big featherbed. He'd found his place in the world right there in Healdton, Oklahoma. His drifting days were over.

She pulled him onto the bed with her and covered his face with kisses. Heat boiled inside her but she knew just the former lawman recently turned farmer who could take care of it. Her dreams had just come true.

Life was good.